...N BALL

Carrots with a Side of Pilaf

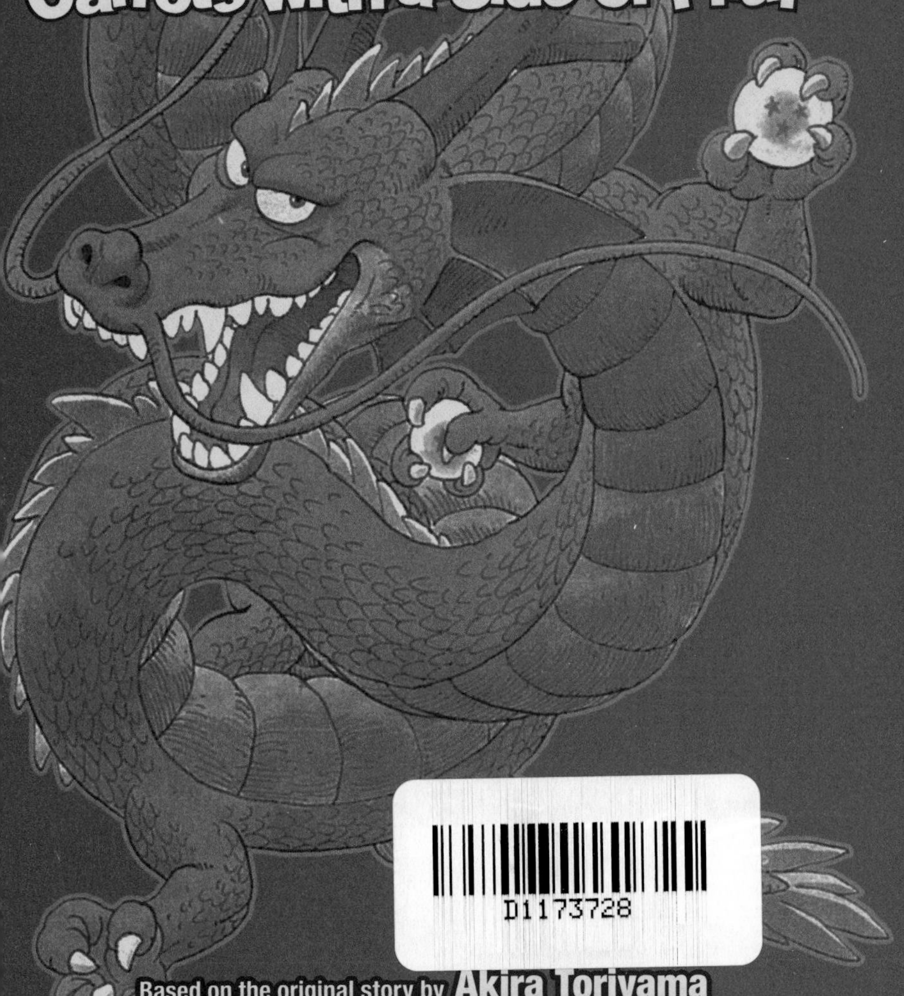

Based on the original story by **Akira Toriyama**

Adapted by Gerard Jones

DRAGON BALL CARROTS WITH A SIDE OF PILAF
CHAPTER BOOK 4

Illustrations: Akira Toriyama
Design: Frances O. Liddell
Coloring: ASTROIMPACT, Inc.
Touch-Up: Frances O. Liddell & Walden Wong
Original Story: Akira Toriyama
Adaptation: Gerard Jones

DRAGON BALL © 1984 by BIRD STUDIO. All rights reserved.
Original manga first published in Japan in 1984 by SHUEISHA Inc., Tokyo.
This English language chapter book novelization is based on the original manga.
The stories, characters and incidents mentioned in this publication are
entirely fictional.

Sources for page 78, "A Note About the Myth of the Moon Rabbit":

JAn, Deming, Turner, Jessica Andrson, and Yang, Lihui. *Handbook of Chinese Mythology.*
Santa Barbara: ABC-CLIO, 2005.

Davis, Susan E., and Margo DeMello. *Stories Rabbits Tell: A Natural and Cultural History of a Misunderstood Creature.*
Brooklyn: Lantern Books, 2003.

Printed in the U.S.A.

Published by
VIZ Media, LLC
P.O. Box 77010
San Francisco, CA 94107

10 9 8 7 6 5 4 3 2 1
First printing, September 2009

www.vizkids.com   www.viz.com

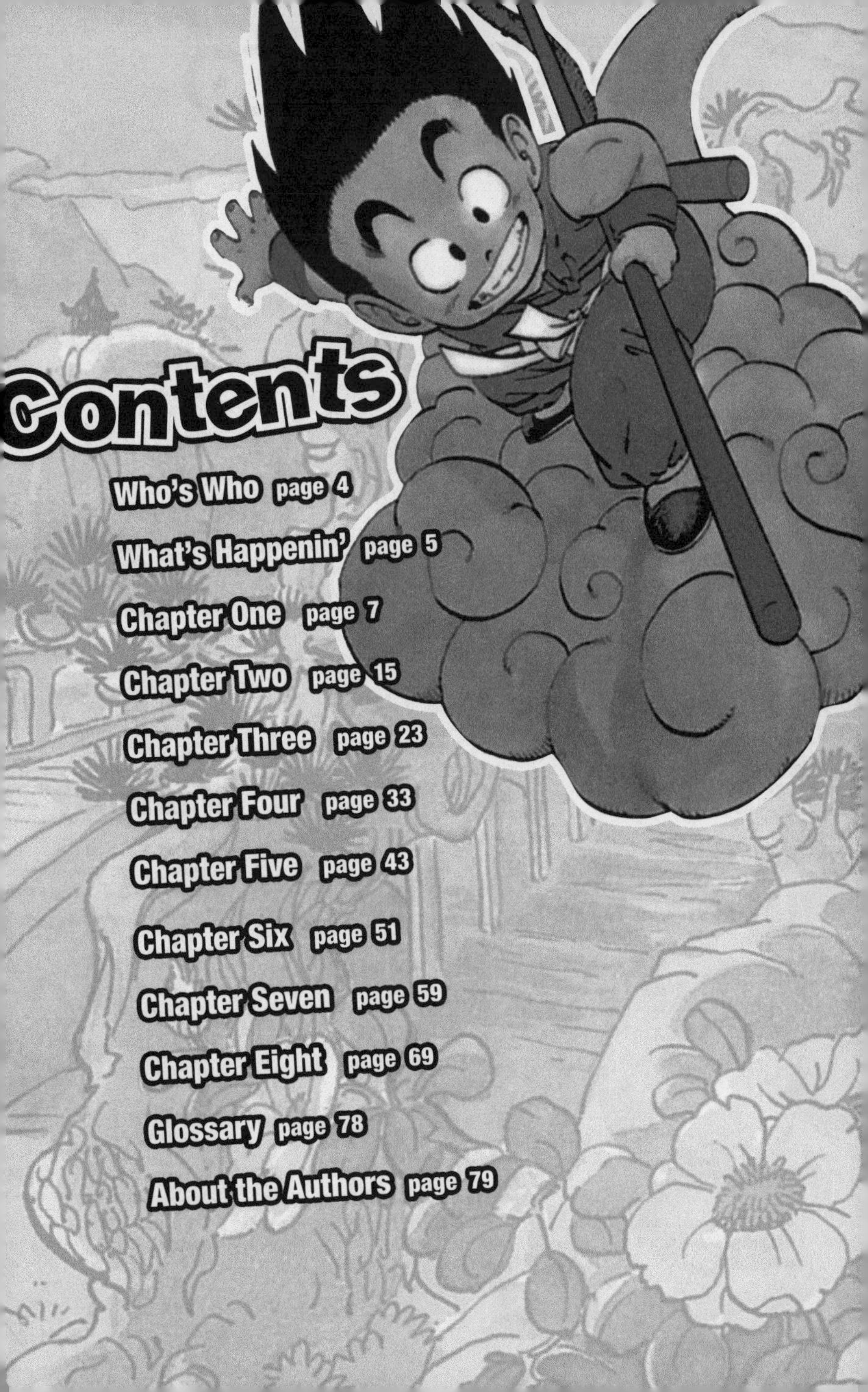

Contents

Who's Who

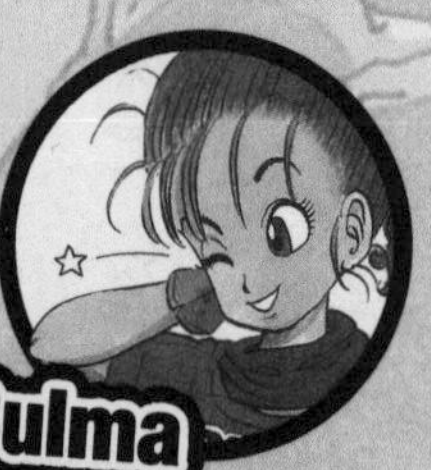

Bulma

Bulma's from the wide world and is a technological genius. She's also a little hung up on her looks, but nobody's perfect. Besides, without her Goku'd still be hanging out in the forest, catching fish with his tail.

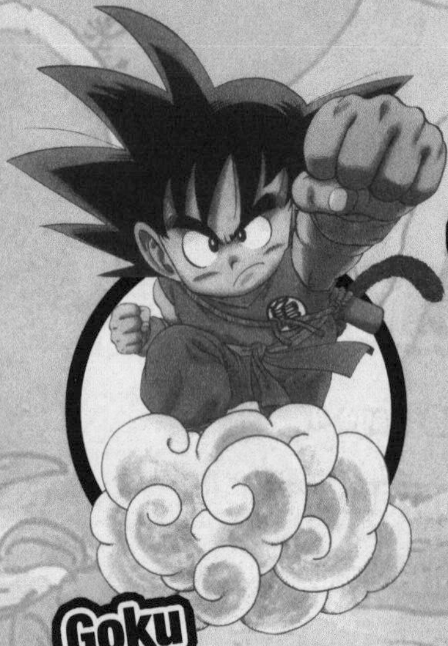

Goku

Since the death of his grandfather, Goku has lived alone, deep in a forest completely cut off from the wide world. He's small for his age but unnaturally strong. And what's with that tail?

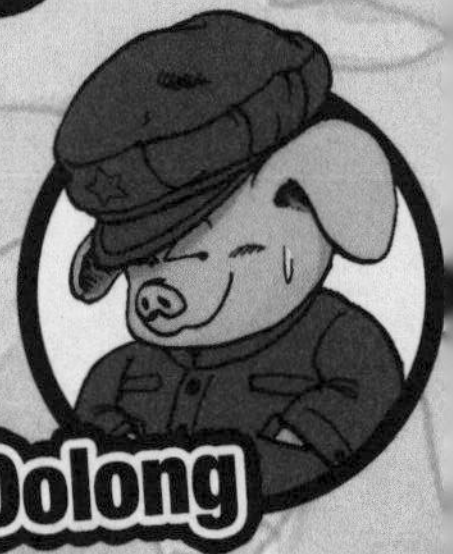

Oolong

Can you count on this shifty little piggie? Not by the hair on your chinny-chin-chin!

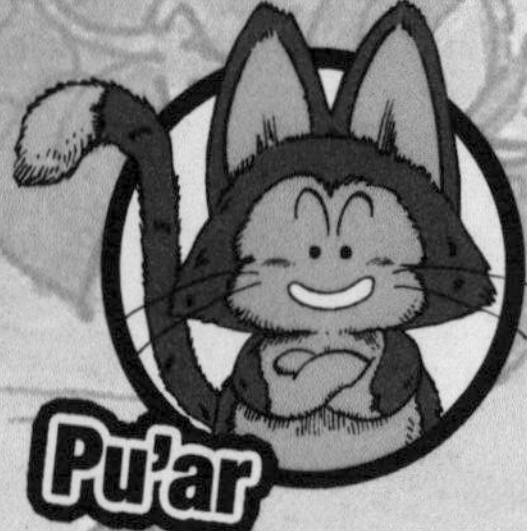

Pu'ar

Pu'ar is Yamcha's shape-shifting sidekick.

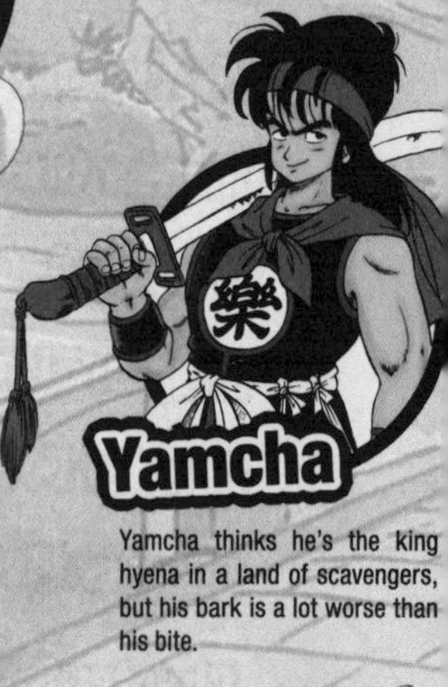

Yamcha

Yamcha thinks he's the king hyena in a land of scavengers, but his bark is a lot worse than his bite.

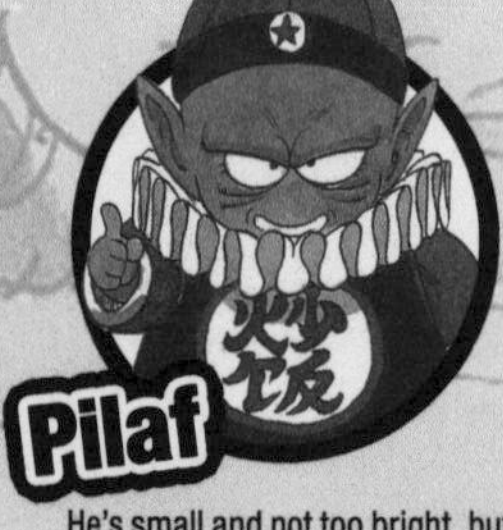

Pilaf

He's small and not too bright, but he might just bumble into world domination.

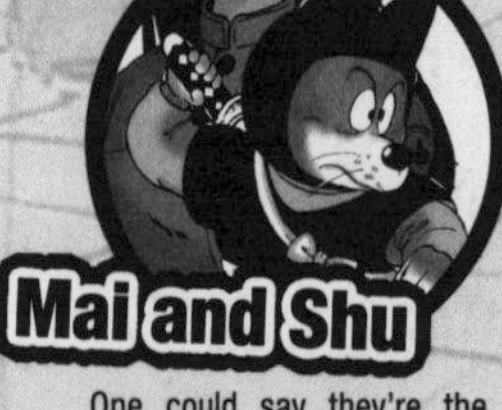

Mai and Shu

One could say they're the brains behind Pilaf's whole operation. But one wouldn't say that to Pilaf.

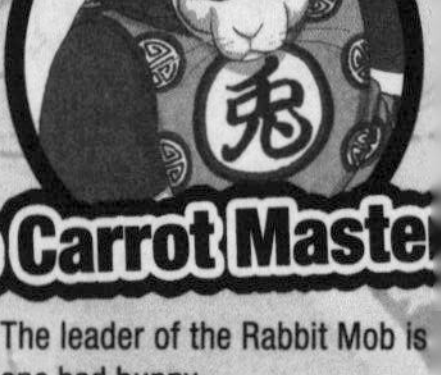

The Carrot Maste

The leader of the Rabbit Mob is one bad bunny.

What's Happenin'

We last saw our heroes zooming away from the ruins of Fry-Pan Mountain, the former home of the formerly fearsome Ox King. What happened to the Ox King's lair? In an amazing and unexpected display of raw power, Master Roshi rocked the rock with his bare hands! But not before shaming the Ox King into giving up his wicked ways. Now Goku, Bulma, and Oolong (with Yamcha and Pu'ar in hot pursuit) are headed into lands unknown.

There's sure to be adventure just around the corner!

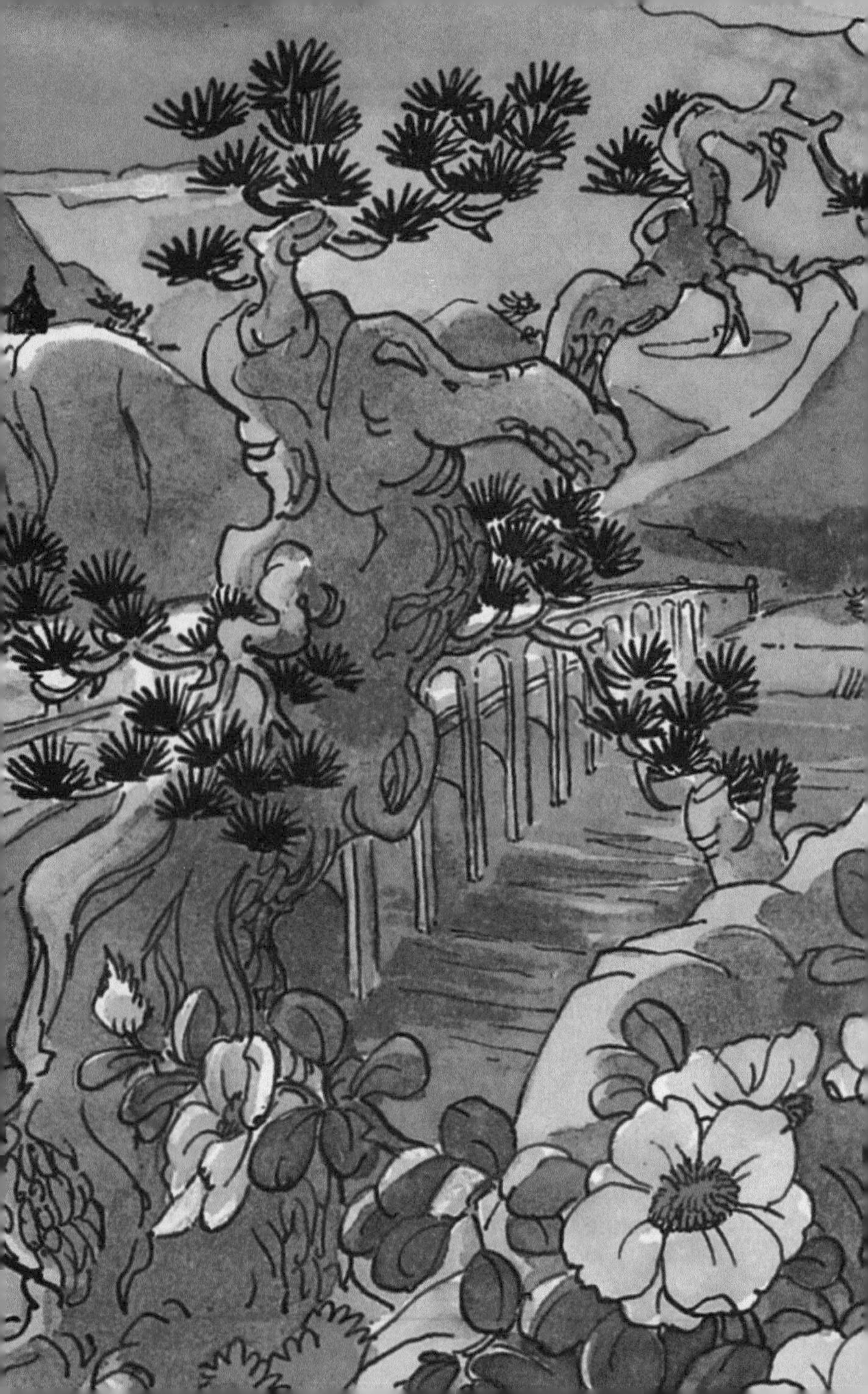

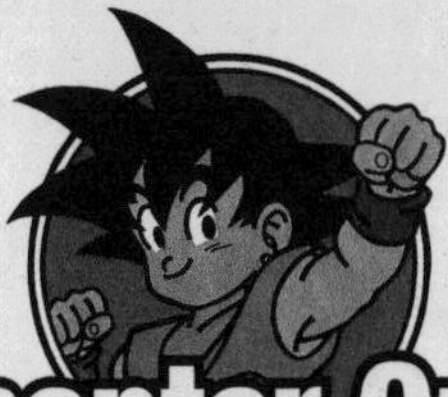

Chapter One

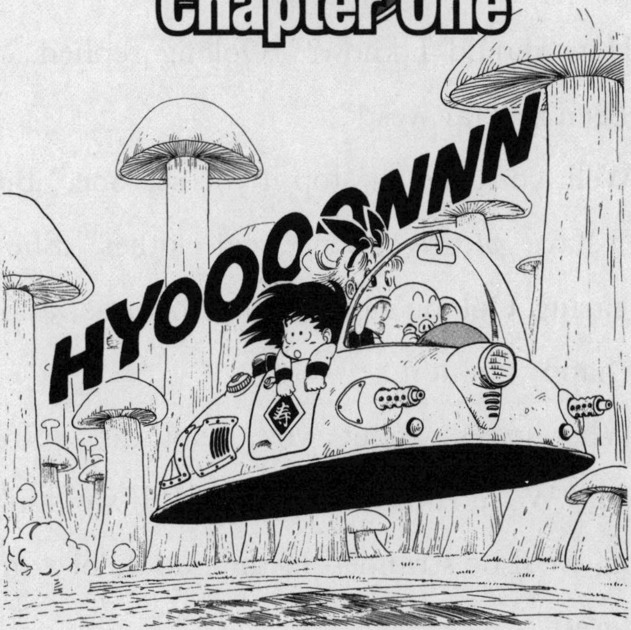
HYOOOONNN

Goku, Bulma, and Oolong rode west in search of *Isshinchu*, the seventh and final Dragon Ball.

The rocks and plants around Fry Pan Mountain gave way to a very different landscape. The ground was perfectly flat, and all around mushrooms grew as large as trees. Their caps blotted out the sky.

"What a weird place this is!" Goku said.

"Hey Oolong," Bulma asked, "is there a village or anything around here?"

"How should I know?" Oolong replied. "I've never been this far west!"

"Well, you'd better stop if you see one," Bulma said. "I have *got* to get some real clothes." She was still wearing Oolong's old bunny costume, and she wasn't happy about it.

"Who cares about your clothes?" Oolong snapped. "We're running out of fuel. If we don't fill up soon, we'll be stranded in the middle of a mushroom forest."

As Oolong drove on, Yamcha and Pu'ar followed some distance behind. They planned to steal the Dragon Balls as soon as Bulma collected them all. Then Yamcha would summon the dragon god and make his own wish.

"Don't let them out of your sight!" Yamcha shouted as they zoomed along.

“Aye, aye, sir!” Pu’ar replied.

Up ahead, Oolong drove into a small town. “Civilization!” Bulma cried. “We’re saved!”

As happy as Bulma, Goku, and Oolong were to see the town, the townspeople weren’t quite as happy to see them.

Goku waved hello to a woman on the street. The woman looked at him. She looked as if she might wave back until she saw Bulma. Then she ran away screaming.

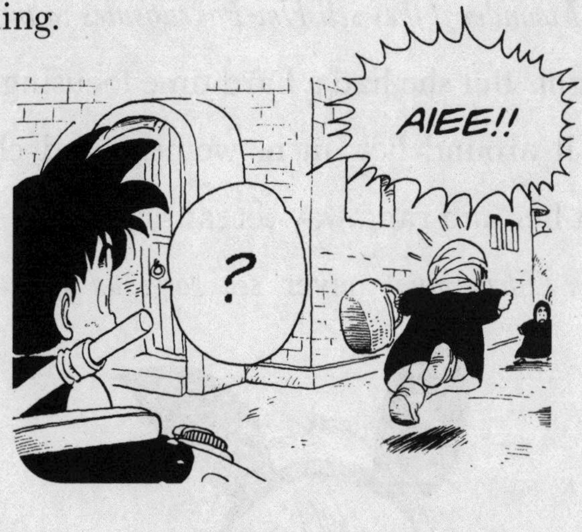
AIEE!!
?

Goku looked at Bulma too. “You don’t look that scary to me,” he finally decided, “but that woman was afraid of you!”

"No way," Bulma said. "She's just never seen anyone so gorgeous before. Beauty like mine can be overwhelming."

Oolong rolled his eyes but didn't say anything. He pulled into a fuel station, and Bulma hopped out of the car.

"I'm going shopping," she called. "Wait for me."

Bulma wandered to what looked like the center of town. *I wonder if they sell Hoi-Poi capsules in this dump,* she thought. But she had a hard time focusing on the stores. All around her, men, women, and children looked at her and ran away screaming.

Wow. They must never see gorgeous girls in this place.

Back at the fuel station, Oolong and Goku waited while the attendant filled the tank of their car.

"Y-your t-t-ank is full," the attendant said finally.

"Thanks," Oolong replied. "You'll have to wait to get paid, though. The one with the wallet'll be back soon."

"N-no, no! *Please*!" cried the attendant, trembling. "It's on the house!"

"On the *house*?"

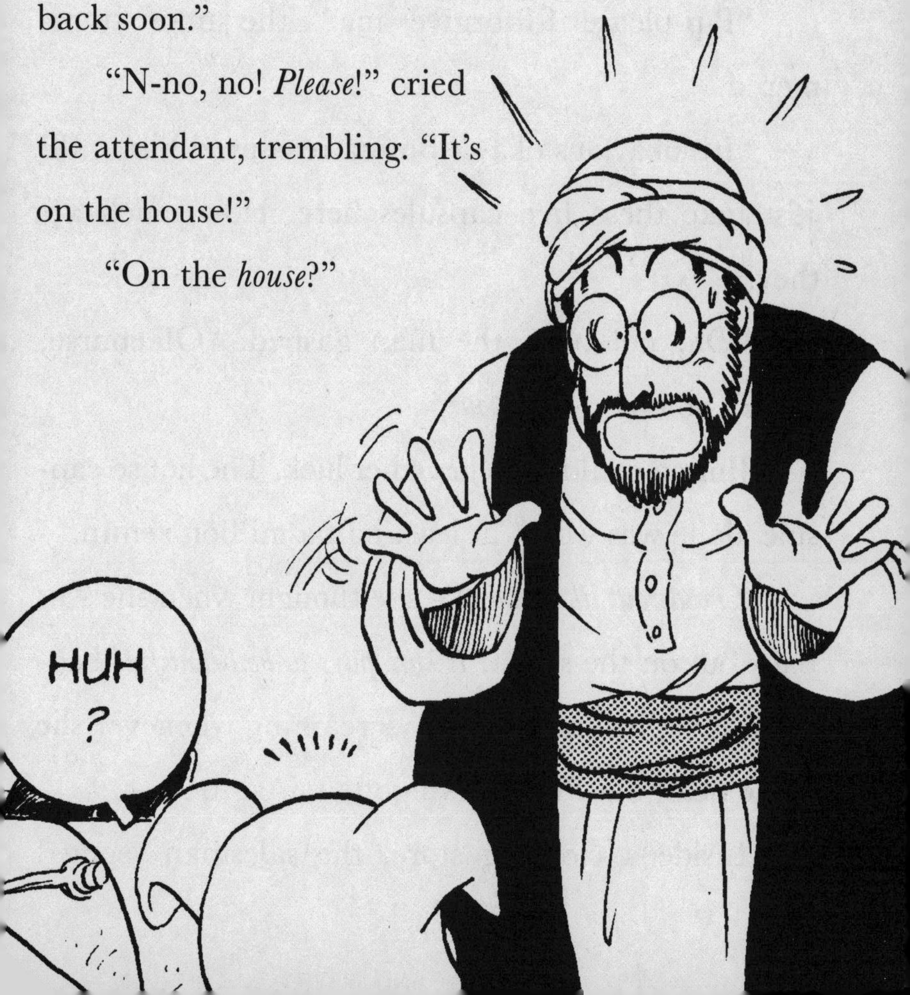
HUH
?

Back in town, Bulma had found a little store that sold Hoi-Poi capsules. The salesman seemed so nervous around her that Bulma almost felt sorry for him.

"You don't have much of a selection, do you?" she said, looking at the small display case.

"P-p-please f-f-forgive me!" the man stammered.

"It's okay, it's okay," Bulma reassured him. "I'll just take these five capsules here. How much are they?"

"Oh, no! No!" the man gasped. "Of course, there's no charge for *you!*"

Bulma couldn't believe her luck. The house capsule alone was worth at least half a million zennii.

I made out like a bandit! she thought when she was back out on the street. *It sure pays to be beautiful!* People were still running away screaming whenever she came near, but Bulma had gotten used to it.

Inside a clothing store, the salesman seemed

just as nervous as the capsule clerk had been. He bowed and stammered as he showed Bulma all the clothes he had for sale.

"This is the best you've got, huh?" she said, trying on an outfit that looked a bit like something a genie might wear.

"Y-yes," sputtered the salesman.

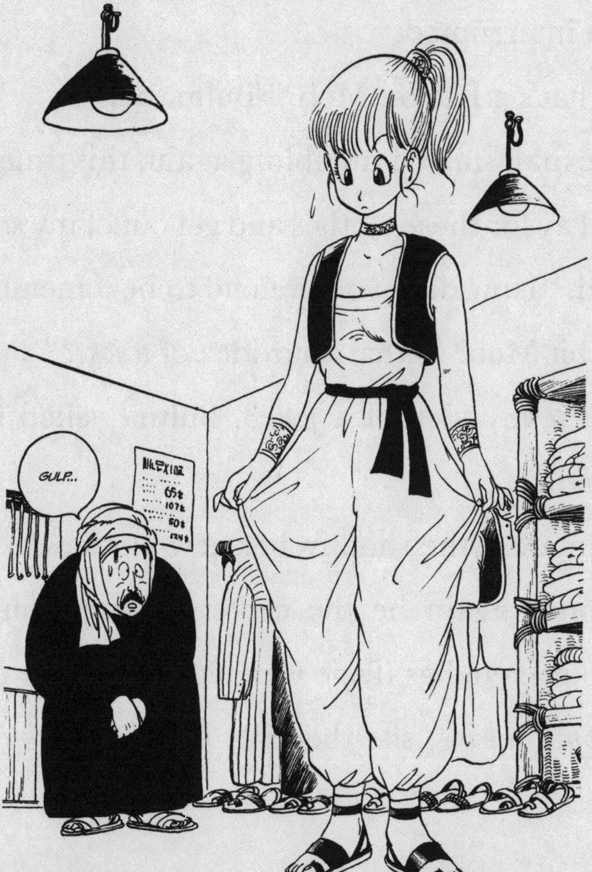
GULP...

"Well, I guess anything's better than that bunny costume."

"Costume?" the man asked. His nervousness was suddenly gone. "That was a *costume?*"

"Yes, of course!" Bulma replied. "You don't think I'd—"

"You mean you're *not* part of the Rabbit Mob?" the man interrupted.

"What's a Rabbit Mob?" Bulma asked.

The man started trembling again, this time with anger. "Pay for those clothes and get out of my store!" he yelled. "How dare you pretend to be a member of the Rabbit Mob? Is that your idea of a *joke?*"

"*You're* my idea of a joke," Bulma yelled back. *What a weirdo.*

Bulma left the shop in her new clothes, expecting to once again be the center of attention. But now people acted as if she weren't even there. *Everyone's stopped staring,* she thought. *What the heck's going on here?*

Chapter Two

"Hey guys, thanks for waiting," Bulma said when she got back to the fuel station. "The strangest thing just–"

"Did you get food?" Goku interrupted. "I'm starving!"

"Here you go," Bulma said, handing Goku a snack. "But listen, I–"

"Hey," Oolong said, pointing down the street. "Check out those creeps."

Coming toward them were two very large men in black coats, goggles, and...bunny ears. The short one grabbed an apple from a street vendor's cart.

"*Blech!*" he spat after taking a bite. "You call these apples?!" He threw the fruit at the vendor and kicked his cart over.

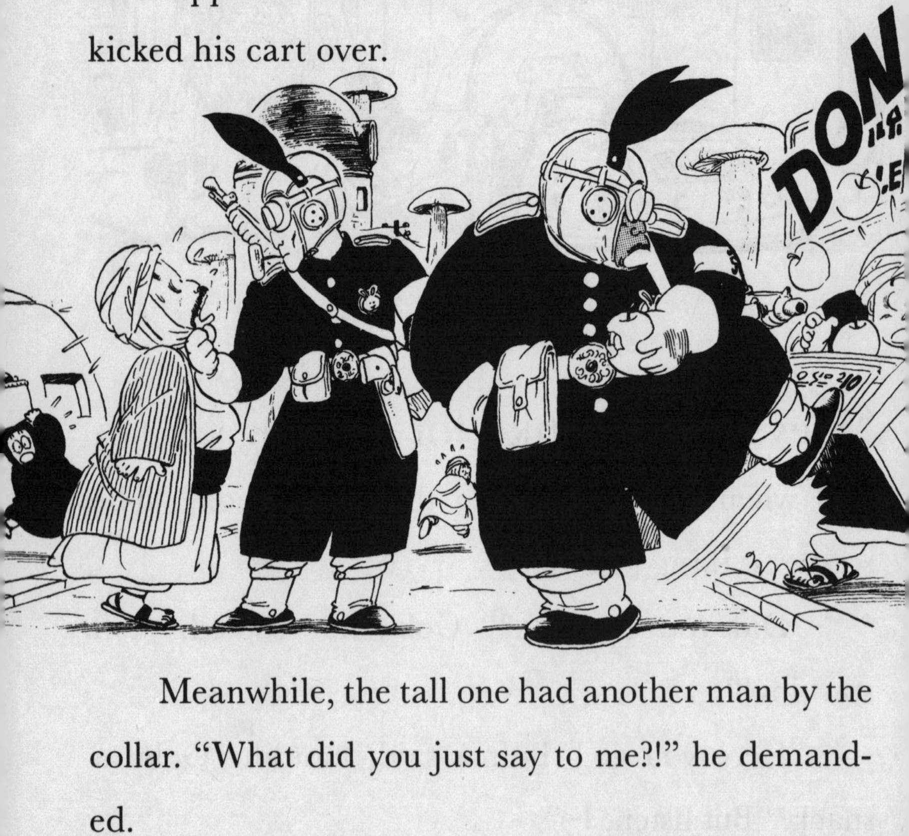
DON

Meanwhile, the tall one had another man by the collar. "What did you just say to me?!" he demanded.

"N-nothing, sir! Nothing!" stammered the collared man.

As Oolong, Bulma, and Goku watched, the men attacked anyone who came near them.

"Who gave you permission to cross in front of me, boy?" one of them yelled.

"P-p-please forgive him, sir!" gasped the boy's mother. "He's just a child!"

"Teach him some manners!" the man barked, and pushed the woman into the street.

"Whoa!" Oolong gasped. "Even *I* was never that much of a bully!"

"Now I know why everyone ran from me before," Bulma said. "Come on, let's get out of here."

Unfortunately, the guys in the bunny ears had a different idea.

"Hey, you!" the short one yelled at Bulma.

"You're kinda cute. Why don't you hang out with us for a while?"

"First of all," Bulma snapped, "I'm more than

just *kinda* cute. Second, there's no way I'm going anywhere with you."

"Oh-ho!" laughed the tall one. "You must be new around here. No one says no to the Rabbit Mob!"

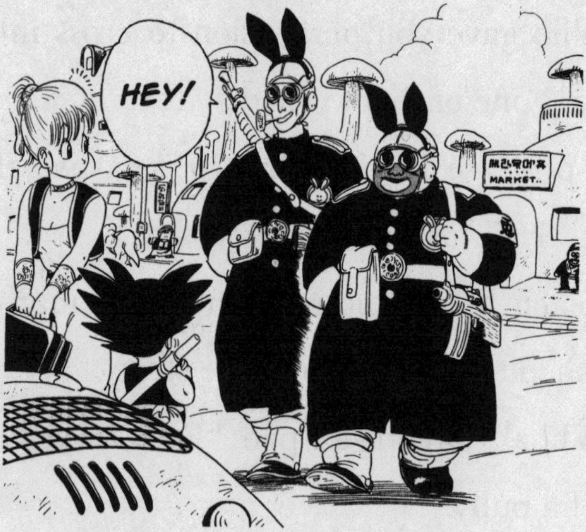
HEY!
MARKET..

"Well, allow me to be the first!" Bulma quipped as she got in the car.

"Feisty, eh?" the tall one said, drawing his gun. "I'll fix that."

Bulma didn't even blink.

"See them, Goku?" she said. "They're bad guys. Feel free to beat them up."

"Okay!" Goku said, his mouth full.

"This little kid?" the tall one laughed. "He's gonna beat us up?"

He kept laughing. The short man laughed too. Goku laughed right along with them. Then he drew back and slammed his fists into the tall man's chest. He spun around and kicked the man in the face.

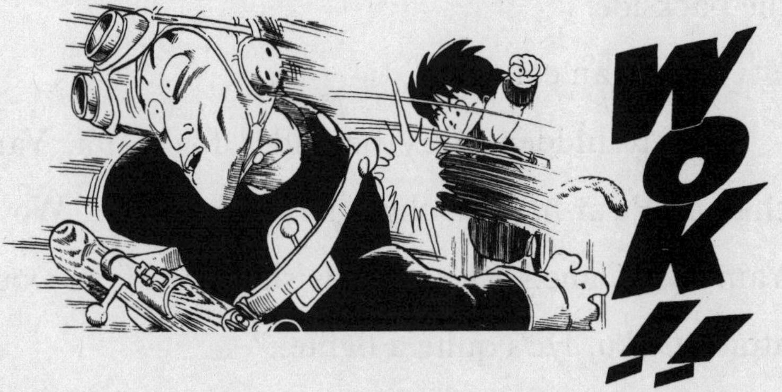
WOK!!

The man crumpled to the ground. He was no longer laughing.

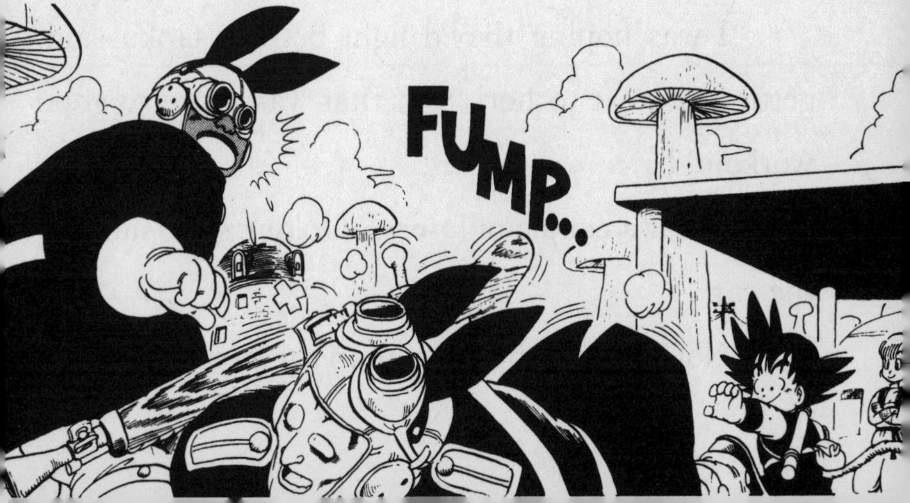
FUMP...

The short man whipped out his gun. "Why, you little—" he snarled.

Before the man could finish, Goku leapt into the air and somersaulted over his head. Just before he landed, he whipped his Noiybo off his back, spun around, and—"HY-AAHH!"—whacked the man on the backside.

The man collapsed.

Safely hidden away behind a fuel tank, Yamcha and Pu'ar had watched the whole scene. "Wow," Yamcha laughed. "I almost wish more idiots would attack Goku. He's quite a fighter."

"Good job, Goku," Bulma said. "Now let's blow this town!"

"I was hoping they'd fight better," Goku said, getting in next to her. "But that was a pretty good workout!"

"What a couple of losers," Oolong said, starting the car.

"Not so fast," the short man sneered as Oolong

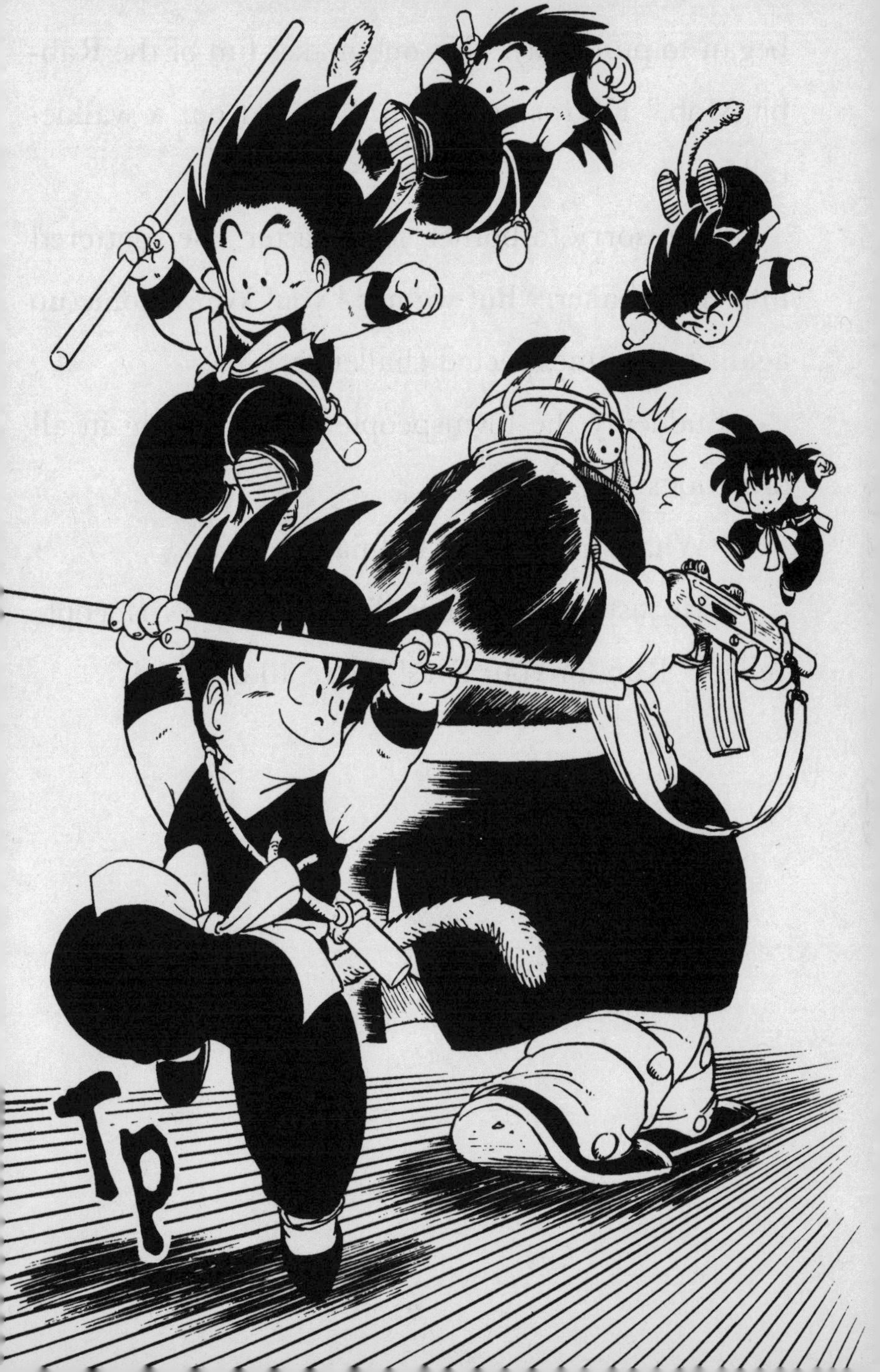
Tp

began to pull away. "No one makes fun of the Rabbit Mob." He rose slowly and pulled out a walkie-talkie.

"I'm sorry to bother you, master," he sputtered into the speaker. "But we need you! We've come up against...an unexpected challenge."

Suddenly the townspeople were running in all directions.

"What's going on?" Bulma asked.

"He just called his boss!" one of the townspeople yelled. "Run for your lives! We're all doomed!"

Chapter Three

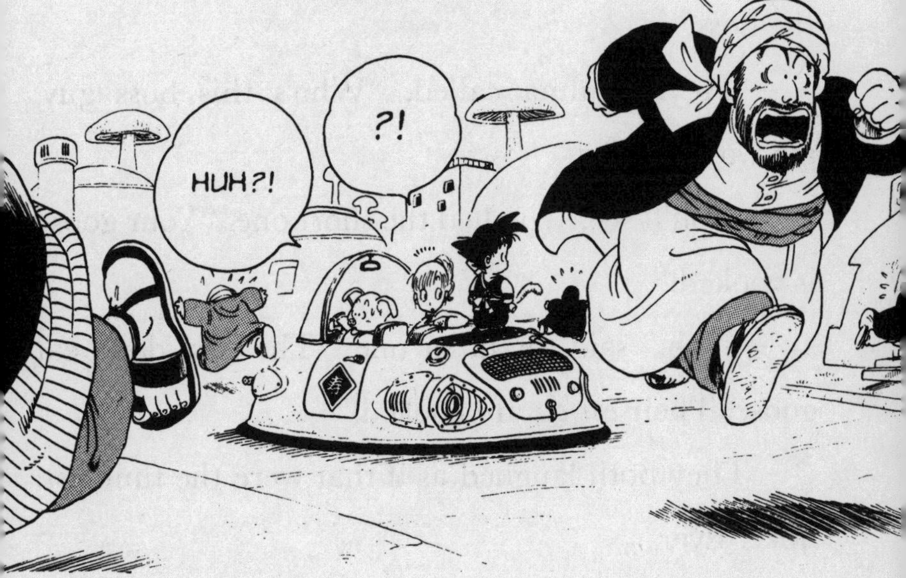
?!
HUH?!

Everyone ran into their houses and slammed the doors behind them.

"Help me think of a reason that this isn't terrifying," Oolong groaned. "Please."

"So rude!" Bulma huffed. "They could've at least thanked us for taking care of those guys."

The rabbit rascals were on their feet now, but the tall one was still struggling.

"That—that *kid!*" he spat, holding his cheek.

"Don't worry," the short one replied. "I called the boss."

"Hey!" Bulma called. "Who's this boss guy, anyway?"

"You'll see," laughed the short one. "Your goose is cooked!"

"Nah," said the taller one. "The boss don't eat goose. Their *carrots* are cooked!"

They both laughed as if that were the funniest. Joke. Ever.

"Carrots," Goku said, and his mouth watered. "I'm still hungry!"

"I don't want to be a carrot!" Oolong yelled. "Let's get out of here!"

"Why should we have to leave?" Goku asked. "We didn't do anything wrong."

"Do you think the boss of some criminal mob

cares if you did anything wrong?" Oolong snapped.

While Oolong and Goku argued, a little car pulled into town. It was shaped like a bunny, long ears, tail, and all. When the bunnymobile came to a stop, the door swung open. Out stepped a chubby rabbit in dark glasses.

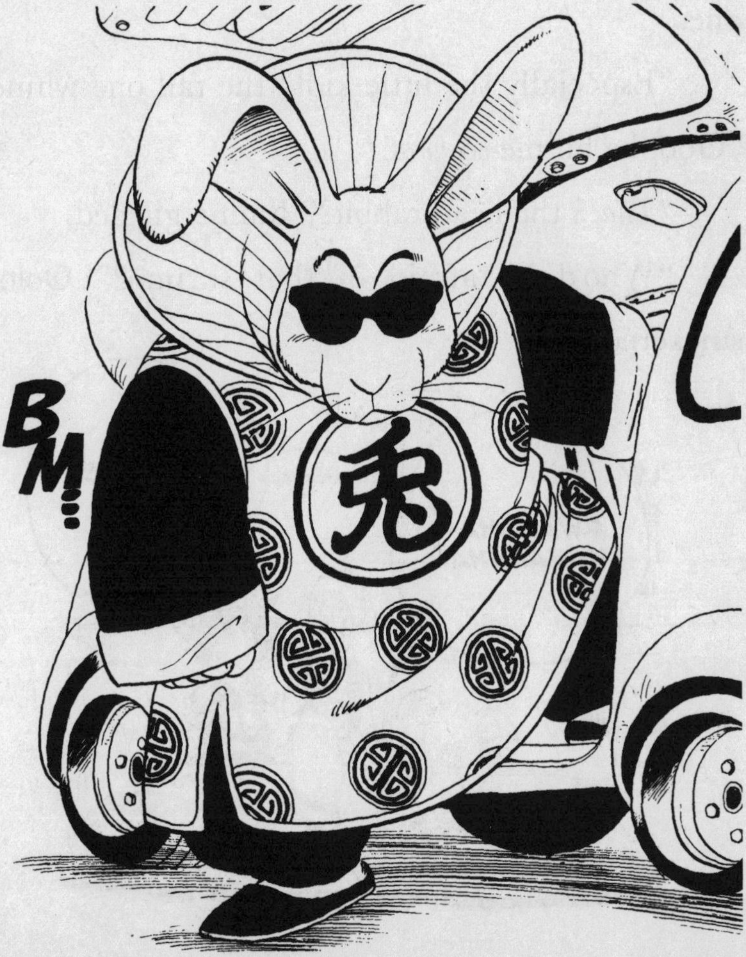
BM!

"Master, master, master!" yelled the tall bunny bully.

"Quit yer cryin'," the bunny boss sneered. "Where's the trouble? I don't see anybody but a girl, a pig, and a kid."

"That's them! That's them!" cried the short one.

"Especially the little kid!" the tall one whined. "Ooo, he hit me so *hard*!"

"*That's* the head rabbit?" Bulma giggled.

"Who'd be afraid of that shrimp?" Oolong snickered.

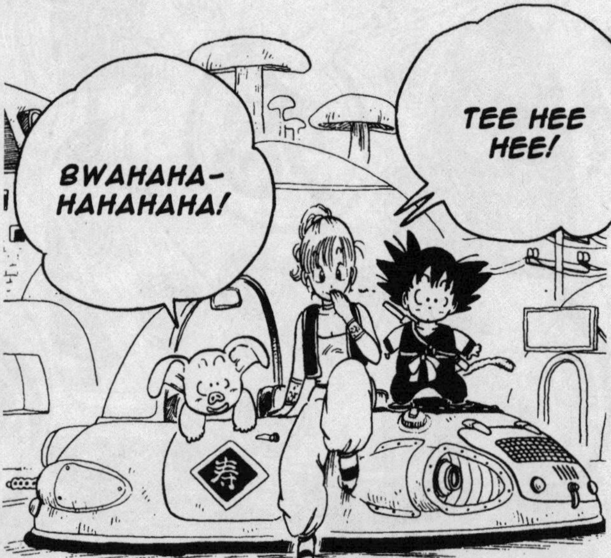
TEE HEE HEE!
BWAHAHA-HAHAHAHA!

For a long moment, the rabbit boss just stared at Bulma, Oolong, and Goku. Then Bulma giggled again.

"Something funny?" the rabbit boss asked coolly.

Without waiting for a reply he leapt up, flipped...

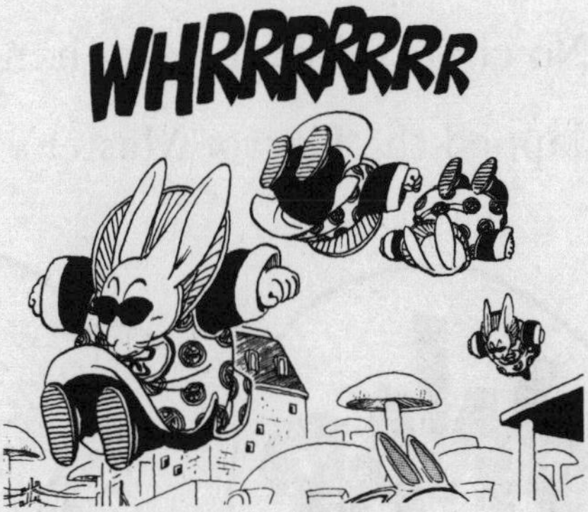
WHRRRRRRR

... and landed right in front of Bulma.

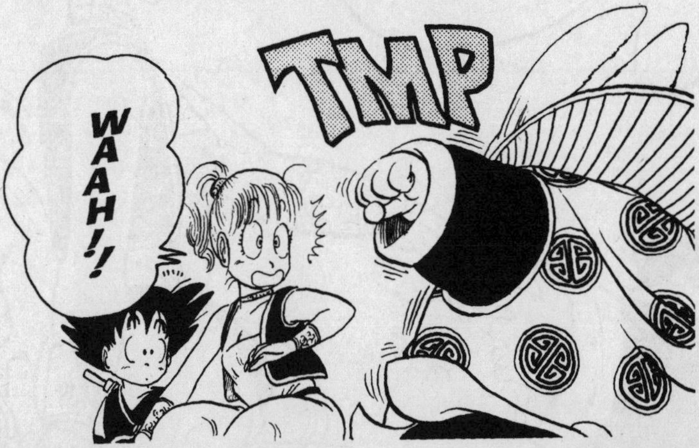
TMP
WAAH!!

"It's not nice to laugh at people," said the bunny boss. "Especially people you haven't met. Nice to meet you," he said, and held out his hand

"I know that rabbit!" Yamcha whispered to Pu'ar. "That's the Carrot Master! If she touches him, she's done for!"

Bulma looked confused for a second, then she chuckled. "No chance I'm shaking hands with a rodent." She slapped the Carrot Master's hand away.

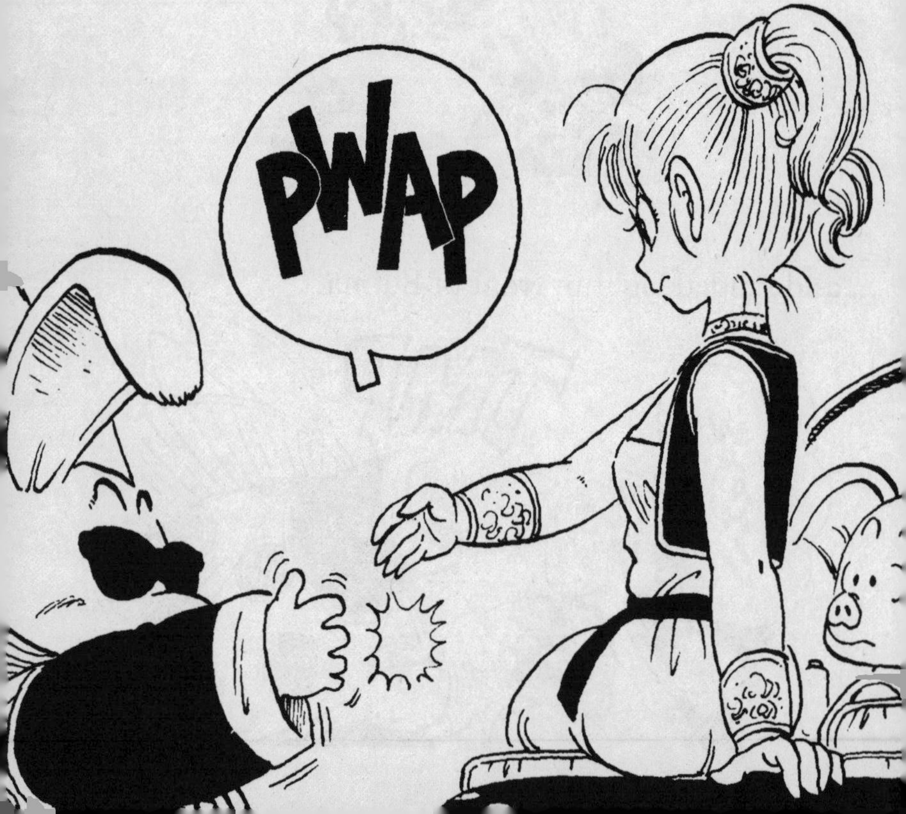
PWAP

The instant she touched him–*POOF!*–Bulma turned into a carrot.

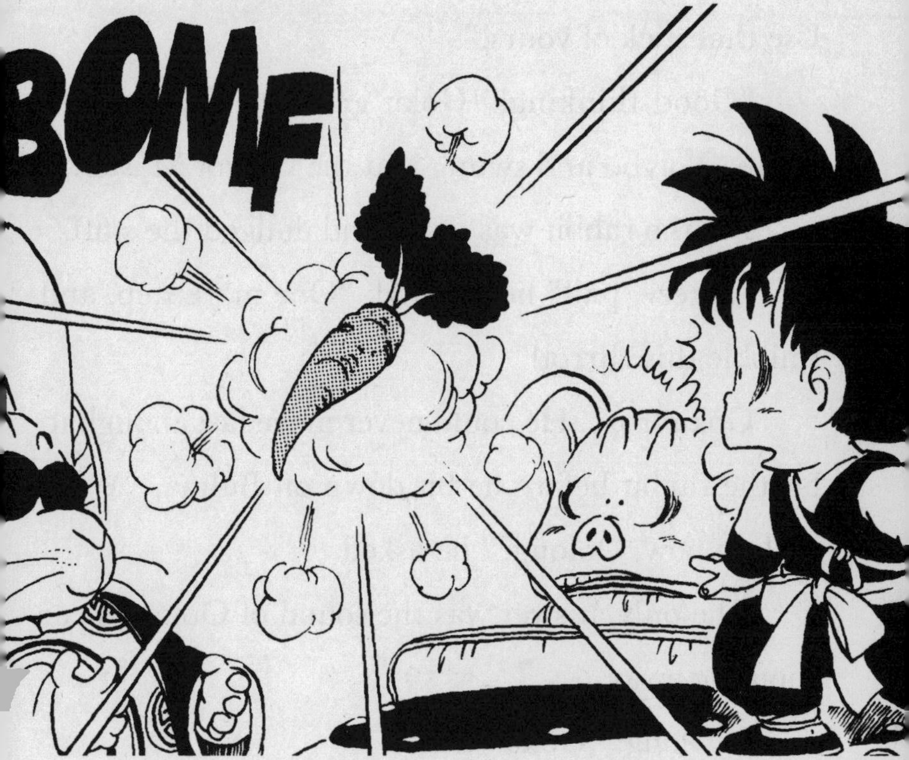
BOMF

The Carrot Master laughed. The bunny bullies laughed with him.

"Change her back!" Goku roared. He jumped out of the car and assumed a fighting stance.

"So you like to fight, eh?" the rabbit said. "Or maybe you've always wanted to be a carrot?"

Goku reached toward the Carrot Master.

"Wait!" Oolong cried. "You can't touch him! Use that stick of yours!"

"Good thinking!" Goku grinned. He whipped out his Noiybo and swung it at the Carrot Master.

But the rabbit was quick and dodged the staff.

"Freeze, pal!" he shouted. "One more step, and I nibble this carrot!"

Goku froze. He could never move fast enough to hit the rabbit before he bit down on Bulma. "What do I do now, Oolong?" he asked.

The only answer was the sound of Oolong's car zooming away.

"Oolong!" Goku yelled.

"Sorry!" Oolong called as he disappeared. "This isn't my problem!"

"Nice friends you got, kid," The Carrot Master laughed. "You could use some better ones. What do you say, boys? How about playing with the little tyke?"

The rabbit roughnecks grinned and pushed up their sleeves. "Time for a little payback, kid," the tall one laughed.

Goku could only stand there as the men came closer and closer.

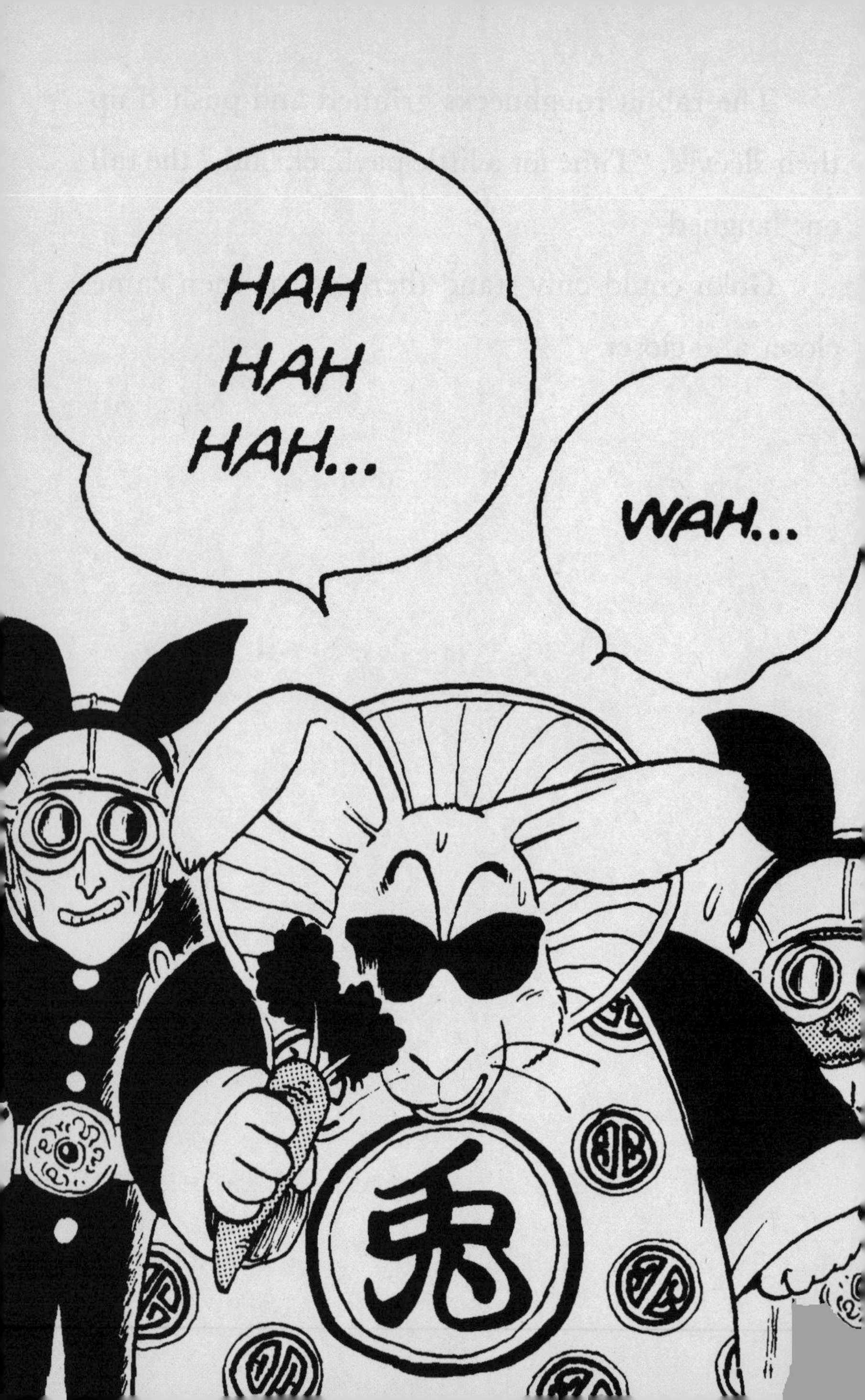
HAH HAH HAH...
WAH...

Chapter Four

WOK
BONK
ZUNK
SHUK
CLONK

From their hiding place, Yamcha and Pu'ar watched Goku take a beating.

"We've got to help him and save the girl," Yamcha hissed, "or they'll never be able to find the last Dragon Ball. Pu'ar! Snatch that carrot!"

"Yes, sir!" Pu'ar said. And–*POOF!*–the little cat changed into a bird. He darted toward the Carrot

Master and, before the bunny could react, snatched the carrot out of his furry little hand.

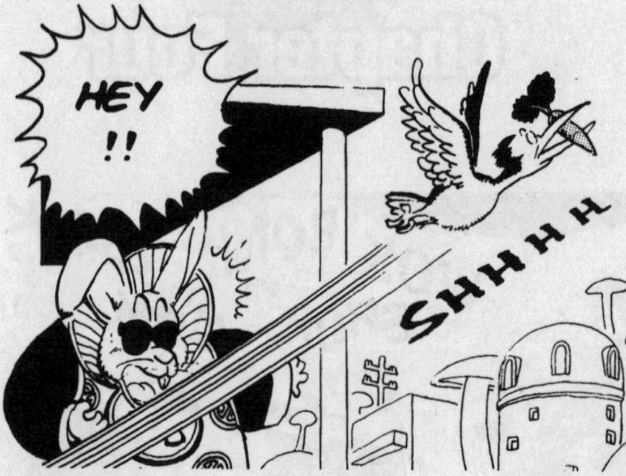
HEY !!
SHHHH

"Get that bird!" yelled the Carrot Master. But before his men could make a move, Yamcha sprang out of hiding and took them down.

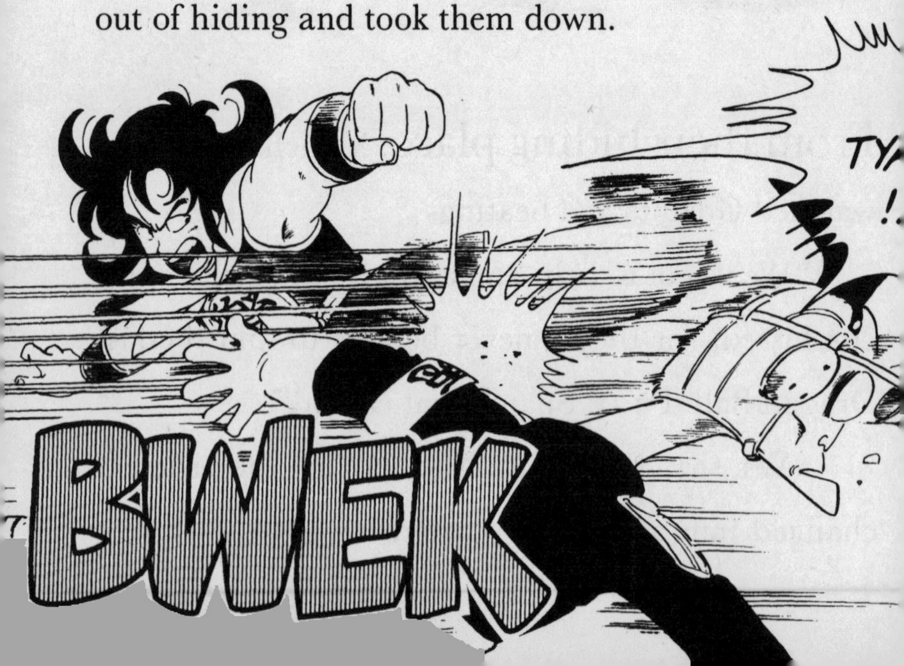
BWEK

"Now," Yamcha roared at Goku, "use your staff to take out that rabbit!"

"Hey, I remember you!" Goku grinned. "What're you doing here?"

"We can talk about that later!" Yamcha growled. "Take care of the rabbit!"

"Oh yeah!" Goku said. And grabbed his staff.

"Hold it right there, pal!" the Carrot Master sneered. "Without me, you'll never change your friend back to human! Let's make a deal!"

But Goku was in no mood to talk. WHAMM! He slammed his Noiybo on the bunny boss's head.

"Owwww!" yelled the rabbit.

"Okay, here's the deal," Goku said, "change Bulma back and I won't whack with you my staff anymore!"

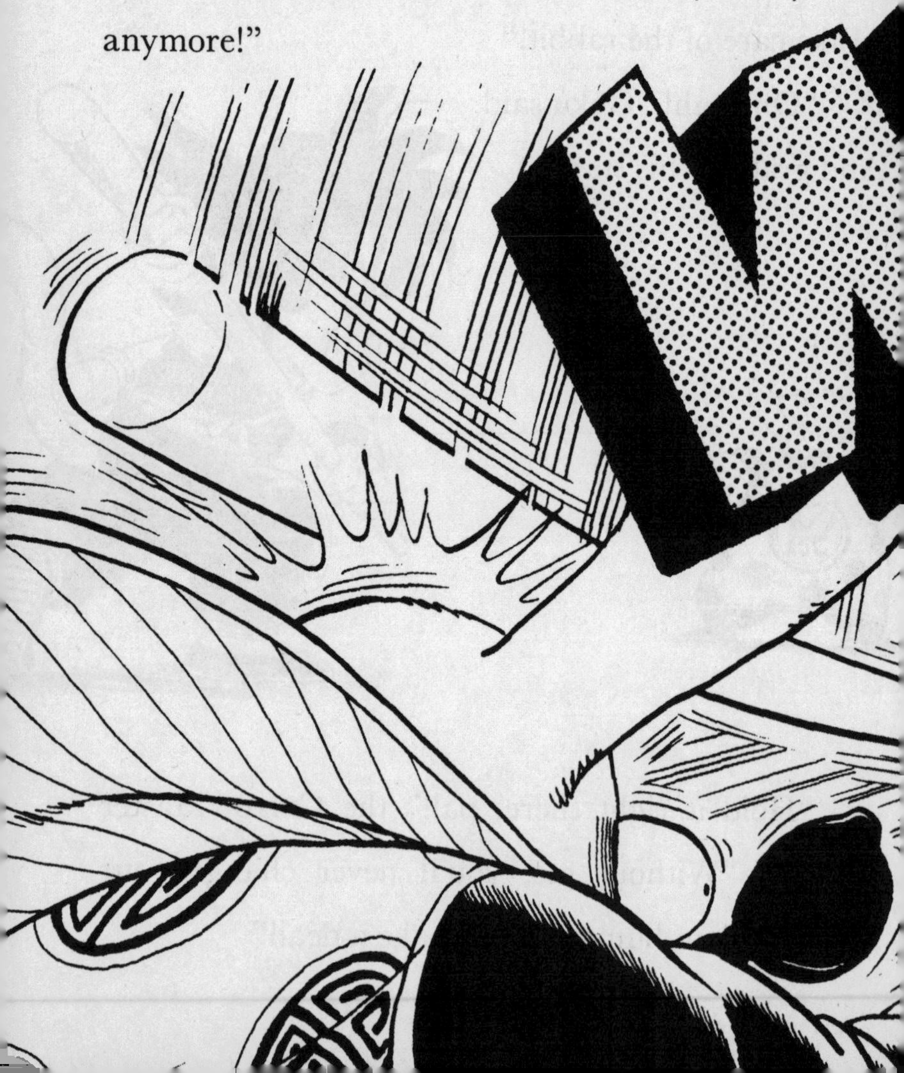

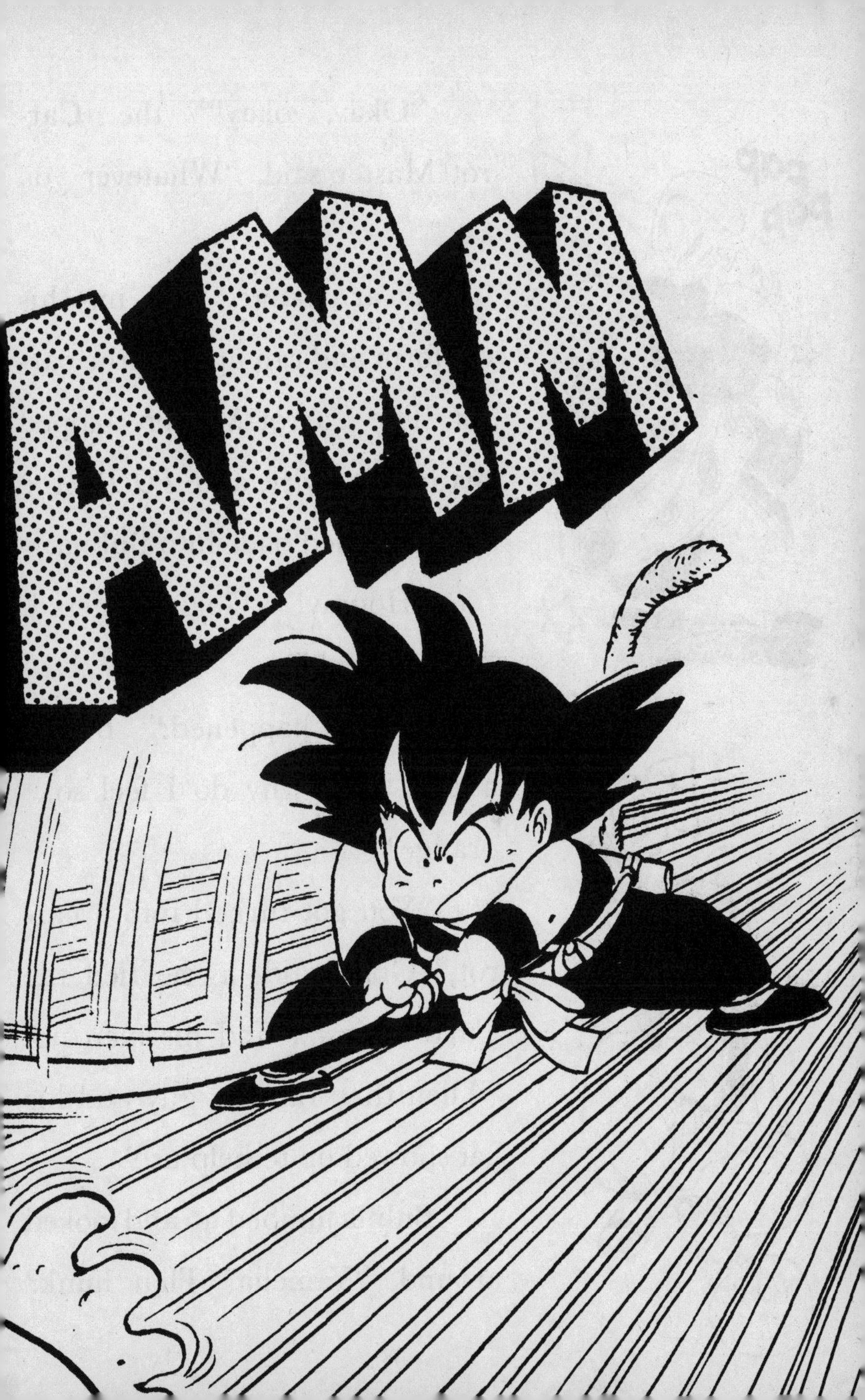
AMM

pap
pap

"Okay, okay!" the Carrot Master said. "Whatever you say."

Pu'ar changed back into his cat form and ran up with the carrot. The Carrot Master clapped his hands twice and—*POOF!*—the carrot turned back into Bulma.

"Hooray!" Goku cheered. "You're back!"

"What happened?" Bulma asked. "And why do I feel so... orange?"

POO

HUH
?

"You got turned into a carrot," Goku said, as he tied the Carrot Master and his men up. "Then that Yamcha guy and his cat showed up to help us!"

Bulma jumped up and looked around. "Yamcha? That hunk?

38

Where is he?"

"That's funny," Goku said. "He was right here a minute ago..."

Yamcha and Pu'ar were hiding behind the fuel tank again. "That was close," Yamcha sighed. "If I'd been a second slower, I'd have been standing right next to a g-g-girl!"

"Lord Yamcha," Pu'ar said, "I can't wait until we can ask that Dragon God to cure your fear of girls!"

"Now, what to do with you three?" Goku said to the Rabbit Mob.

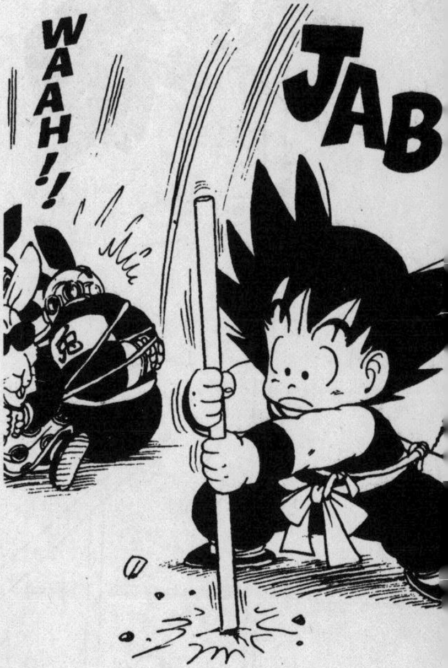
WAAAH!!
JAB

"Have mercy on us!" the short one cried.

Goku thought for another moment then pounded his staff on the ground. "Okay, Nyoibo, you're gonna have to stretch a long way!"

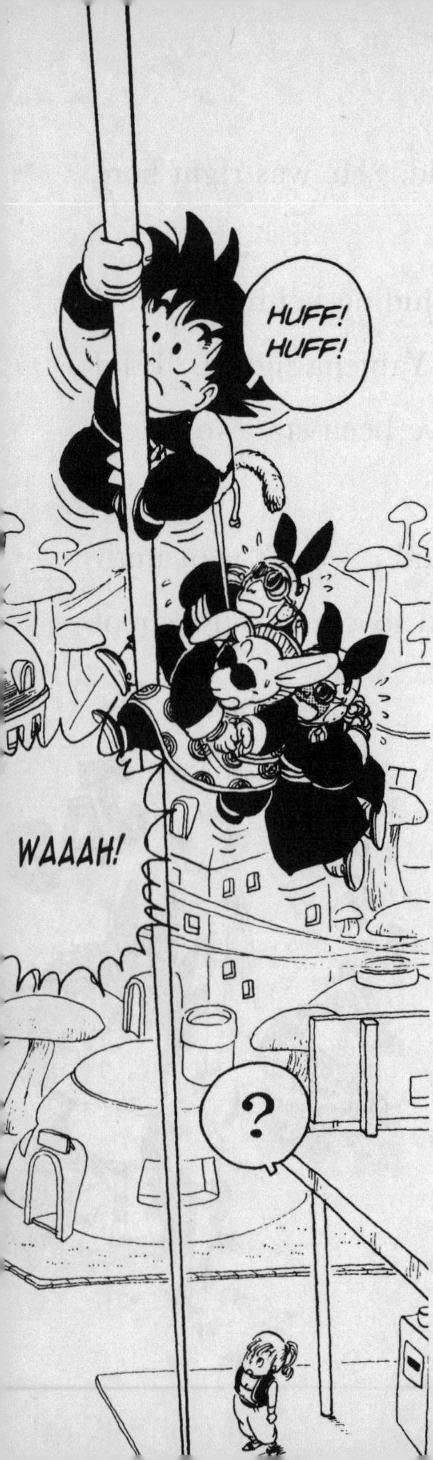
HUFF! HUFF!
WAAAH!
?

The staff grew and grew. Up, up, up it went until its far end disappeared into the sky. Goku slung the Rabbit Mob on his back and started to climb. The townspeople stuck their heads out of their windows and doors to watch the boy carry their enemies away. As Goku vanished into the clouds, Oolong zoomed back into town.

"Is it safe now?" he asked.

"Nice timing, pig," Bulma snapped.

"Hey, I never said I was a hero," Oolong snapped back.

"Oolong! You're back!" Goku cried. He had dumped the Rabbit Mob and was now sliding back down the staff. "What's with you, anyhow? Every time there's danger you run away!"

"What's with *you*?" Oolong snapped. "Every time there's danger, you run right *to* it!"

"Um...Goku?" Bulma asked. "What did you do with the rabbit and his friends?"

"You know the old story about the rabbit in the moon?" Goku said with a smile.

Bulma did indeed know the old tale about the rabbits pounding rice paste on the moon. "Y-you don't mean," she stammered. "You took them all the way to the—"

She stopped herself. *What a ridiculous thought. Surely Goku just left the Rabbit Mob on a rooftop somewhere.* She smiled and shook her head. *Goku couldn't possibly have climbed his staff all the way to the moon.*

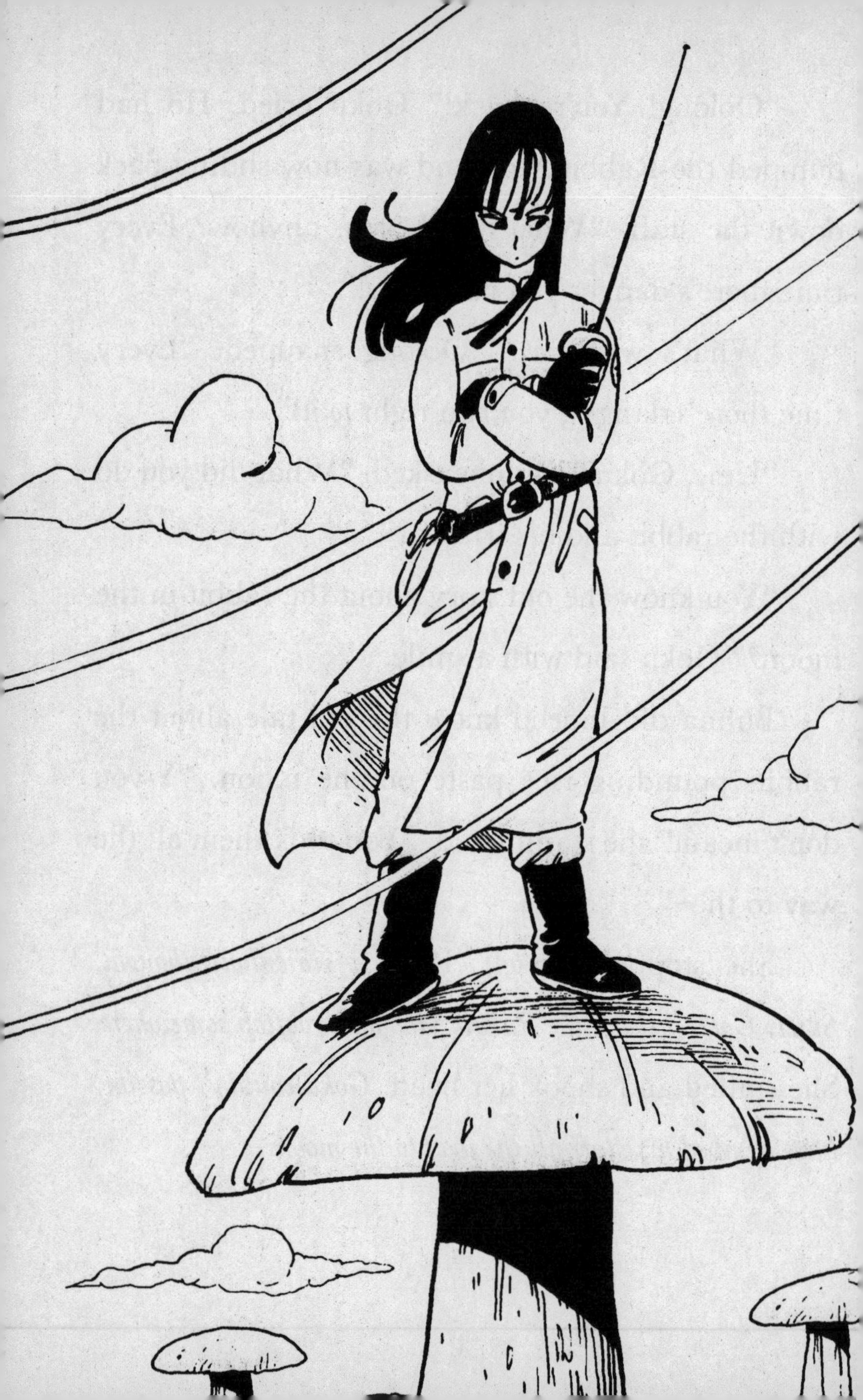

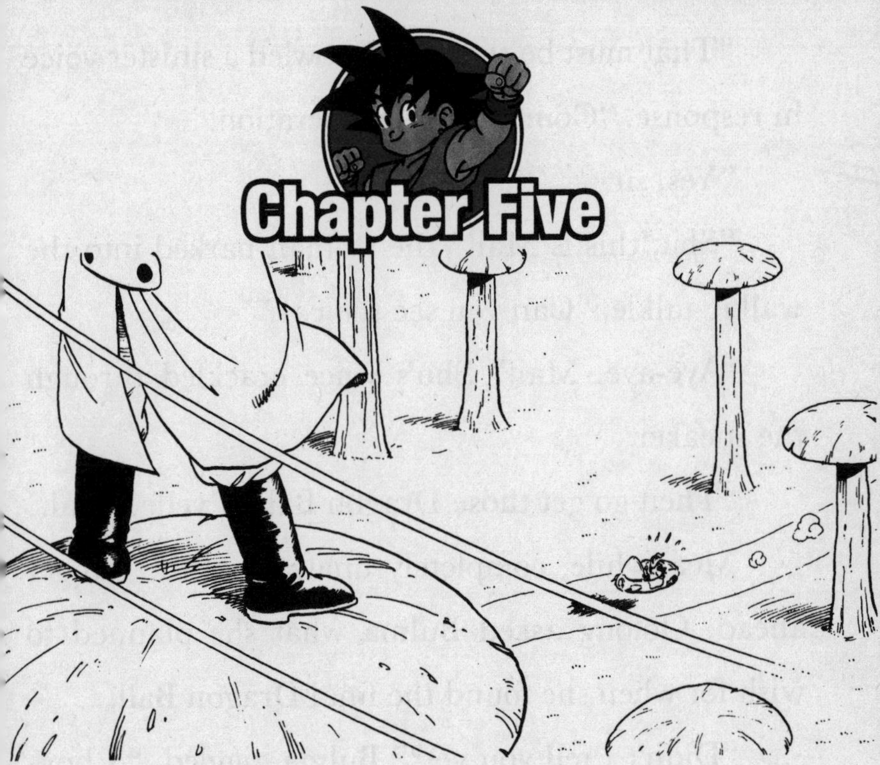

Chapter Five

As they left the town, Bulma's Dragon Radar began to beep loudly again. The last one-star ball was close by! As they raced toward it, a woman watched from the top of a giant mushroom.

"Emperor Pilaf," said the woman into her walkie-talkie, "this is Mai. I am in Area H-15. A car has just passed through."

"That must be the one," growled a sinister voice in response. "Commence the operation!"

"Yes, sir.

"Shu, this is Mai!" the woman barked into the walkie-talkie. "Can you see the car?"

"Aye-aye, Mai!" Shu's voice crackled through the speaker.

"Then go get those Dragon Balls!" yelled Mai.

Meanwhile, completely unaware of the danger ahead, Oolong asked Bulma what she planned to wish for when she found the final Dragon Ball.

"Didn't I tell you yet?" Bulma giggled. "A boyfriend! The world's most awesome boyfriend!"

"A boyfriend?!" Oolong squealed. "You mean I'm going through all this so some girl can get a boyfriend?"

"Not just 'some girl,'" Bulma snapped. "Me. You should feel honored to be part of something so worthy!"

"Worthy my—"

BOOM!

Something struck the car and sent Goku, Bulma, and Oolong flying.

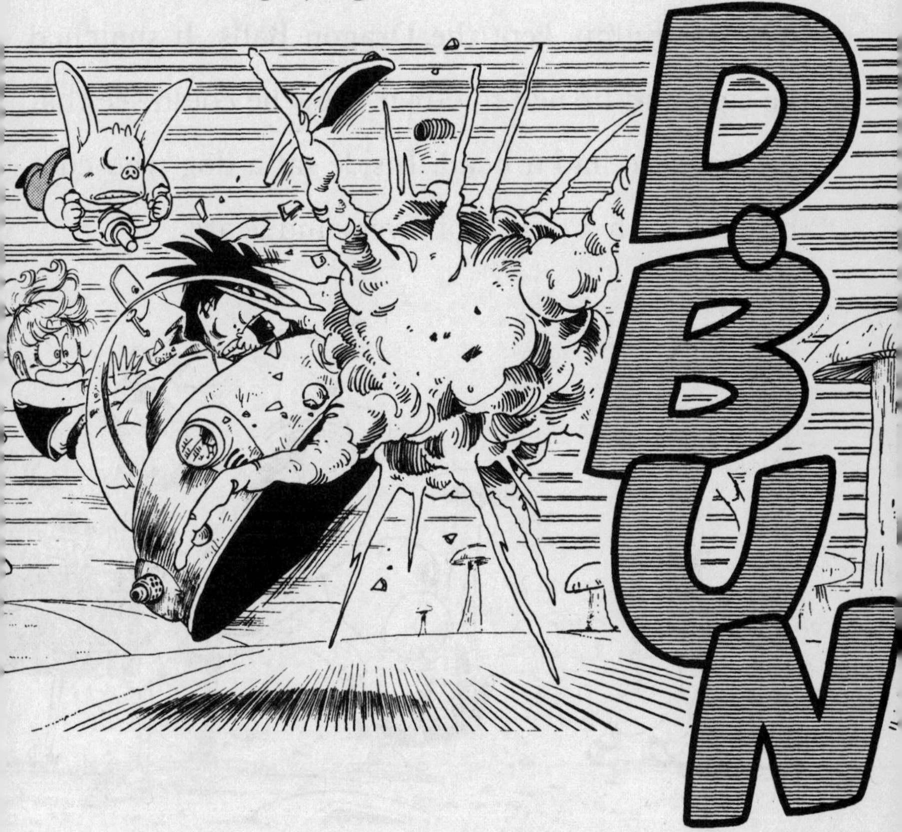
DBUN

With a heavy *CLANG!* an enormous machine landed near the wreckage. Its great bulk was perched on four legs, and it dug through the debris with a monstrous claw. If it could be said that the thing had arms, it had two: the claw and a massive metal cannon.

"Eureka!" the machine cried as it found the case in which Bulma kept the Dragon Balls. It snatched the case and turned to Goku. Now he could see that the machine had a head. Inside sat a dog who controlled it with a bunch of levers and gears.

"Thanks for the Dragon Balls, kid," the dog laughed as he launched the machine into the air. "Sayonara!"

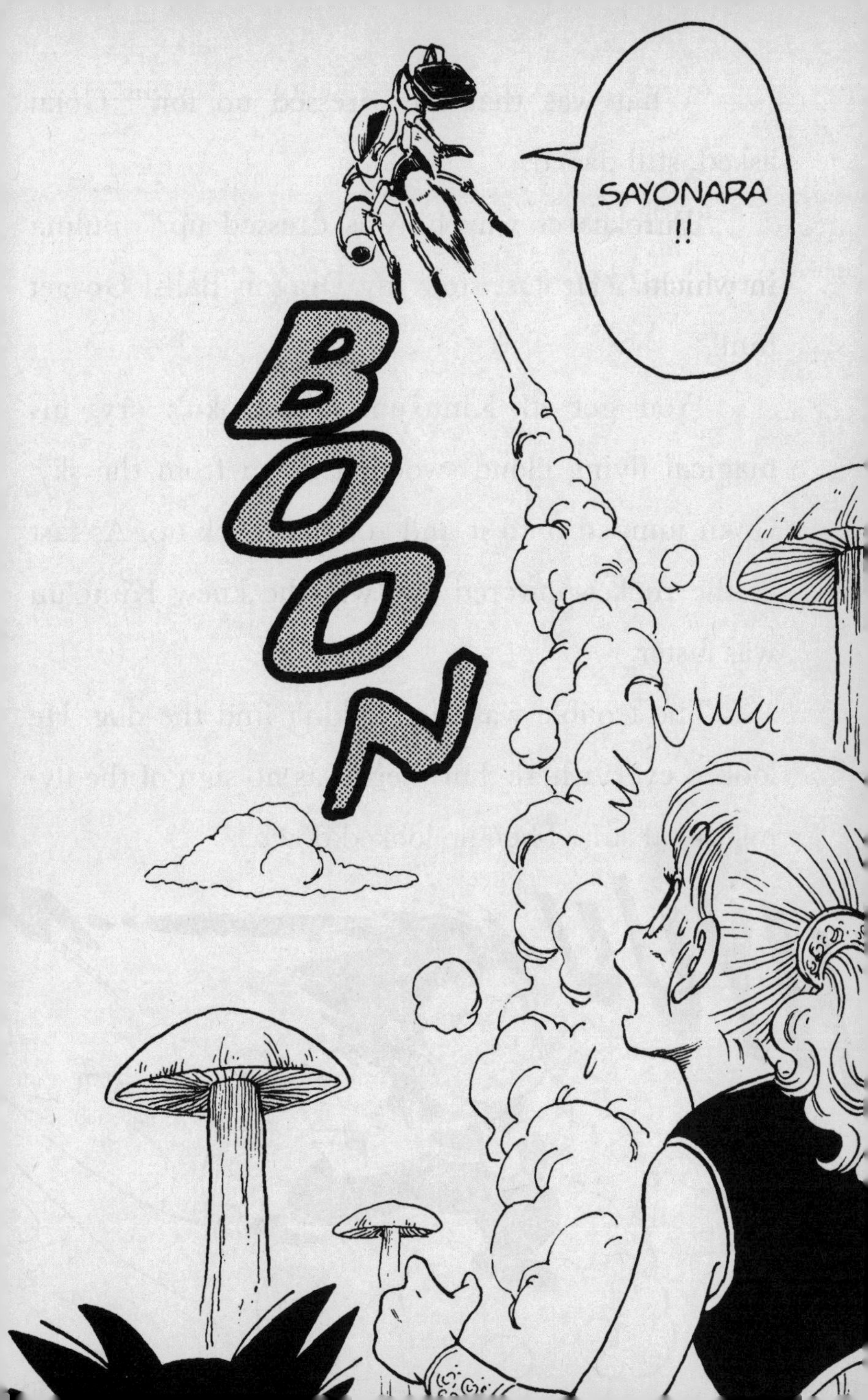
SAYONARA !!
BOON

"What was that guy dressed up for?" Goku asked, still dazed.

"Who cares why he was dressed up?" Bulma screamed. "He just stole my Dragon Balls! Go get him!"

"You got it! Kinto'un!" At Goku's cry, his magical flying cloud swooped down from the sky. Goku jumped onto it and zoomed back up. As fast as the rocket-powered dog was, he knew Kinto'un was faster.

The trouble was, he couldn't find the dog. He looked everywhere, but there was no sign of the flying metal suit. Then he looked down.

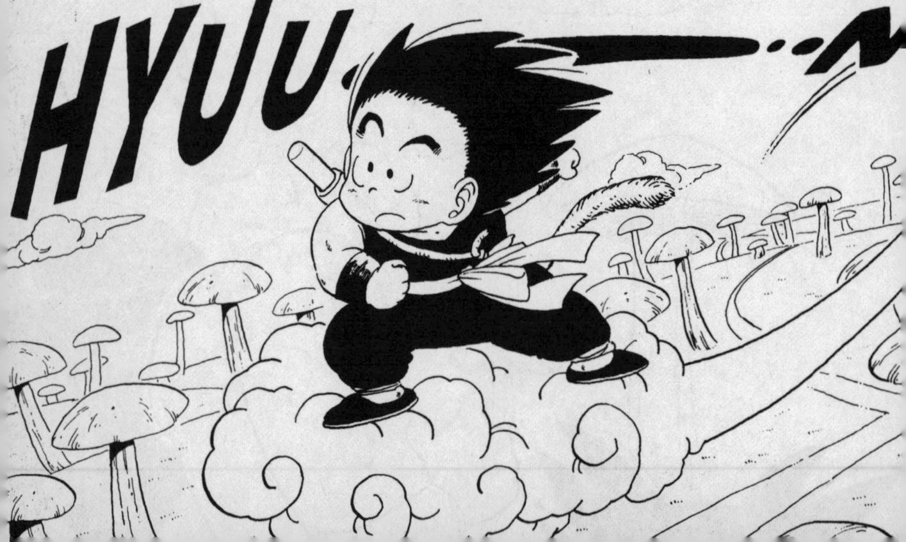
HYUU...N

"There he is!" Goku yelled, and Kinto'un whooshed toward the ground, where the dog's suit stood under a mushroom.

"Hey, you!" Goku called. "What's the big idea of taking other people's stuff?"

There was no answer from the machine. Goku jumped off his cloud and walked toward it, staff in hand. "Well? Say something!" Still no response. Goku jabbed the machine with his staff.

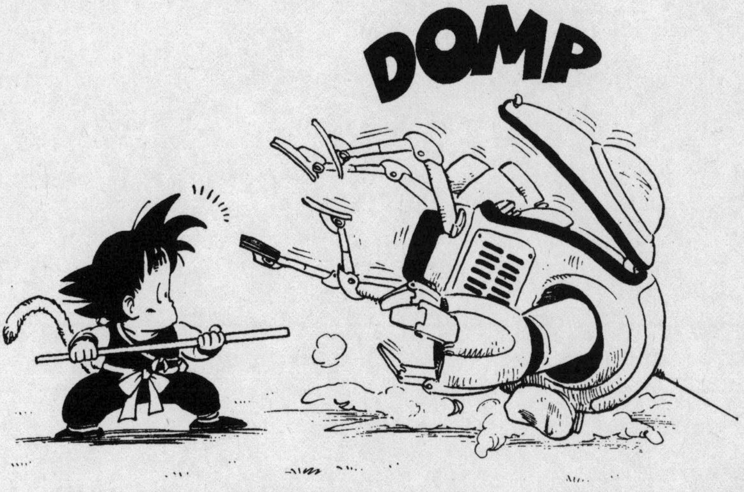
DOMP

The suit teetered and–*WHUMP*–fell to the ground.

He just...died? Goku thought, puzzled. *What a weakling!* But in fact, the machine was empty and the dog was gone—with the Dragon Balls!

Chapter Six

"Did you find him?" Bulma asked urgently when Goku came back.

"Yep, I found him!" Goku said proudly.

"Did you beat him?" Bulma asked urgently.

"I knocked him down!"

"So where are the Dragon Balls?"

"Oh," Goku said, "they're gone."

Bulma fell to her knees and let out a long, long scream. "They've probably got the last Dragon Ball already! Now they've got all seven and I'll never get my wish!"

"They don't have them *all*," Goku said, and pulled the ball that his grandfather had given him out of his pouch.

Suddenly Bulma jumped up and down. "Fools!" she laughed "Thieves! You've missed one! Now we'll use the Dragon Radar to track down your lair...and I will still be the one to claim the dragon's wish!"

"Except how will we get there now that our car's wrecked?" Oolong asked.

"You underestimate me, bucko!" Bulma chuckled. "I bought Hoi-Poi capsules at the last town! I have five of them right..." She stopped chuckling. "Right...in the case...with the Dragon Balls."

And Bulma dropped to her knees and let out another long, long scream.

Yamcha, watching from behind a mushroom,

sighed. "Well, we can't let our Dragon Balls get stolen," he told Pu'ar. "We have to help them, even though it means I'll have to talk to a g-g-g-g-g-g—"

"Be strong, Lord Yamcha," Pu'ar said. "Be strong."

A moment later, Yamcha's car pulled up next to Bulma. Yamcha tried very hard to sound casual. "W-w-well! Wh-what a c-coincidence m-meeting y-you h-h-h-here!" he sputtered.

"Yamcha!" Bulma squealed. "I'm so happy to see you! And for so many reasons!"

"If y-you n-need a ride," Yamcha stammered, "j-just h-h-h-h-h-h–"

"Hop in!" Pu'ar finished.

So Bulma and Oolong hopped in Yamcha's car. Goku rode Kinto'un. Based on the beeping of her Dragon Radar, Bulma told him where to drive. The warrior tried to look straight ahead and pretend that there wasn't a beautiful girl sitting next to him. But Bulma wasn't interested in pretending. She slid over until her arm pressed against Yamcha's.

"Tell the truth, Yamcha," she said sweetly. "You came out here looking for little ol' me, didn't you?" She leaned over and rubbed her cheek against his.

Yamcha screamed. He stomped on the gas pedal so hard that his car nearly crashed into a mushroom stalk.

"Hold on, Lord Yamcha!" Pu'ar yelled. "Hold ON!"

Meanwhile, Mai and Shu—the dog inside the massive metal machine—had returned to Emperor Pilaf's lair.

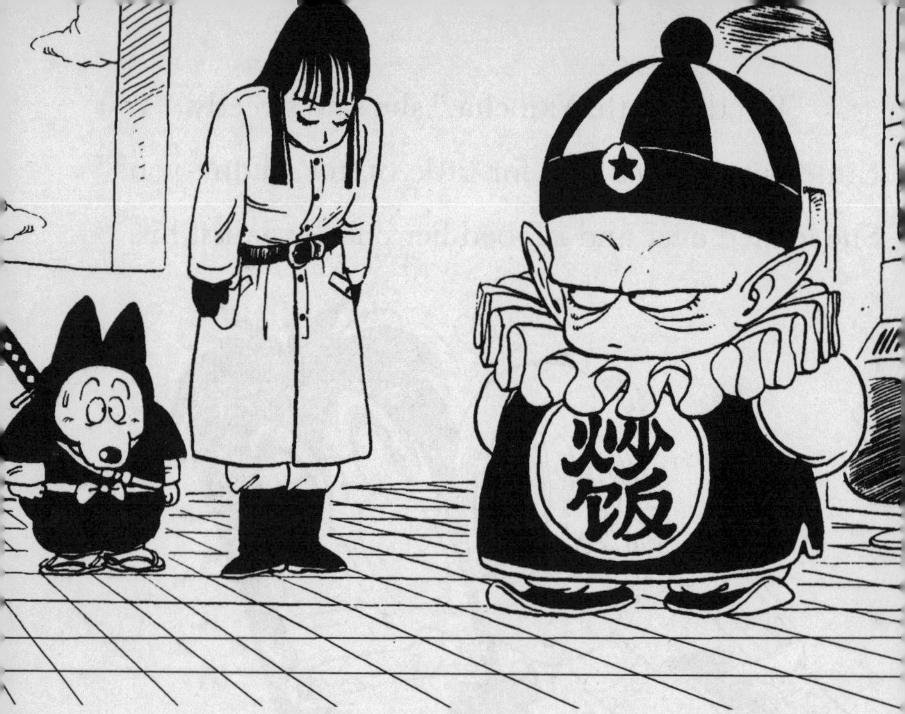
炒饭

"I wish you'd counted the Dragon Balls before you stole them," Pilaf was saying.

"Y-yes, Lord Pilaf," Mai stuttered as she bowed her head. "We are so sorry."

"I guess I wasn't using my noodle, Sire," Shu muttered.

"Well, lucky for you twits, the other ball is heading this way," Pilaf said, looking at his radar screen. "This must be my lucky day. Once I have all the balls, world domination will be mine!"

“They’re here!” yelled Mai, and she switched on a TV screen that showed the grounds in front of the palace. Sure enough, Yamcha’s car was roaring into view.

“Already?” Pilaf asked.

“Shall I set the trap, my lord?” Mai asked.

“That you shall,” the little emperor chuckled. “And soon *I* shall rule the world!”

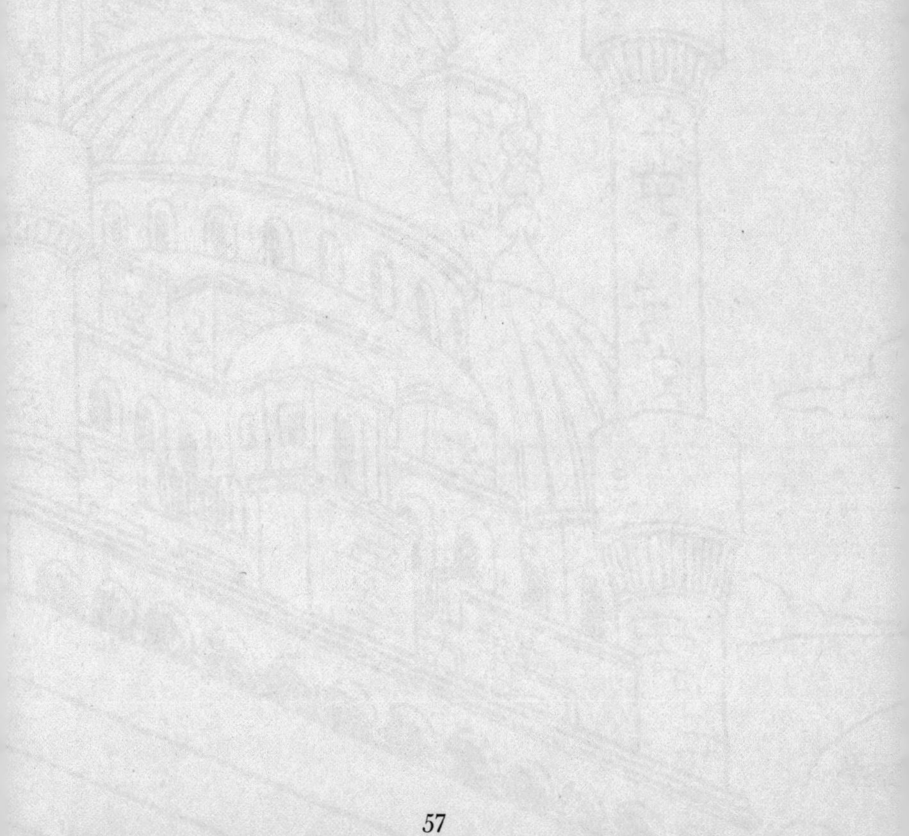

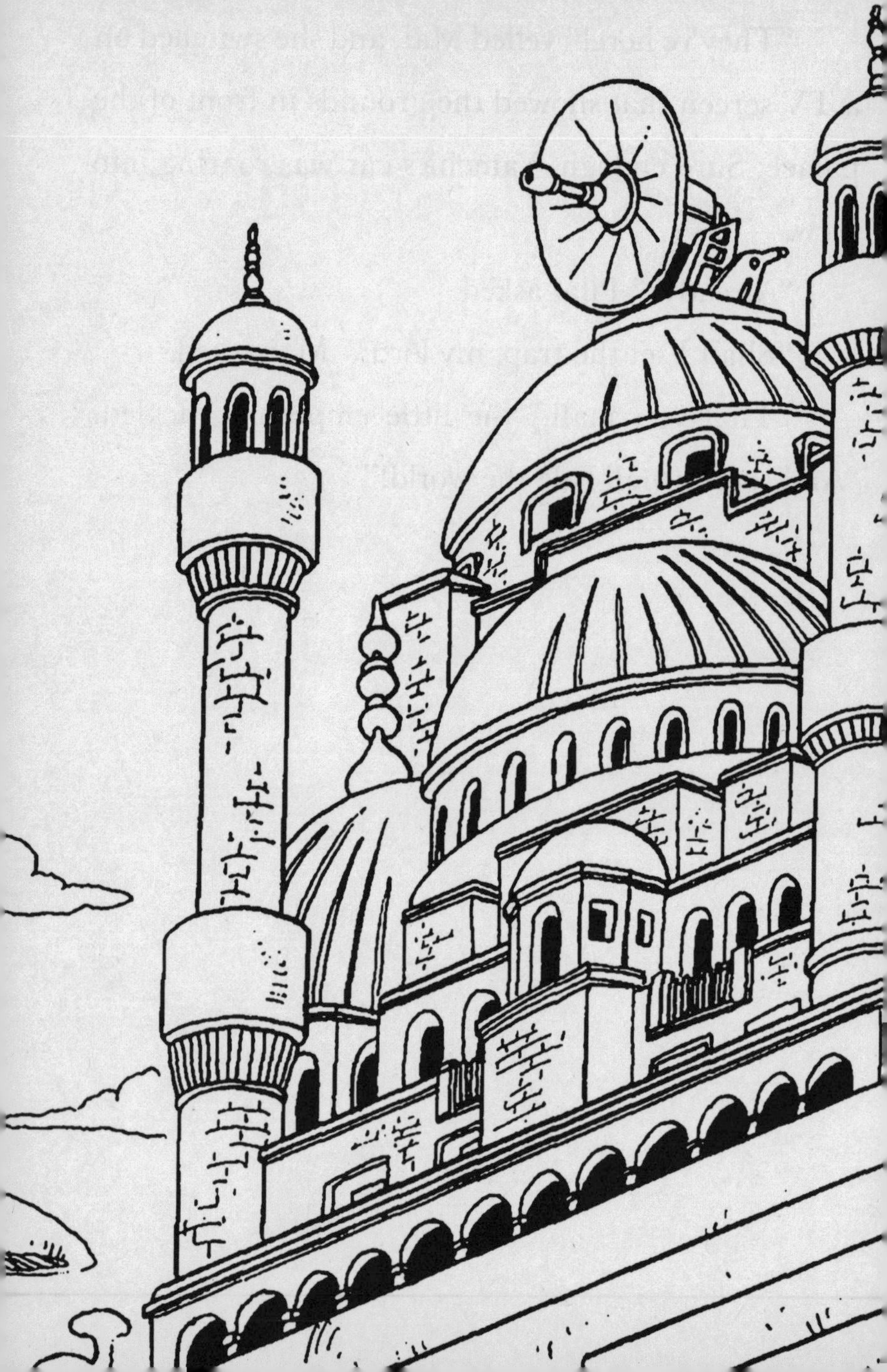

Chapter Seven

Yamcha rolled his car to a stop in front of a set of steep steps that led to a huge palace.

"According to my radar, all six Dragon Balls are in that building!" Bulma gasped.

"How're we gonna get in?" Oolong asked.

As if in response, a door at the base of the steps slid open.

"Alright!" Goku said. "Let's go!"

"Whoa. *That's* not suspicious at all," Oolong quipped.

The door opened onto a dark, narrow tunnel. Goku stayed close to the wall, and Bulma followed. Yamcha was close behind, Oolong and Pu'ar clinging to his leg.

"I don't think we're dealing with ordinary thieves," Yamcha whispered.

"Look!" Goku said. "There's an arrow painted on the floor!"

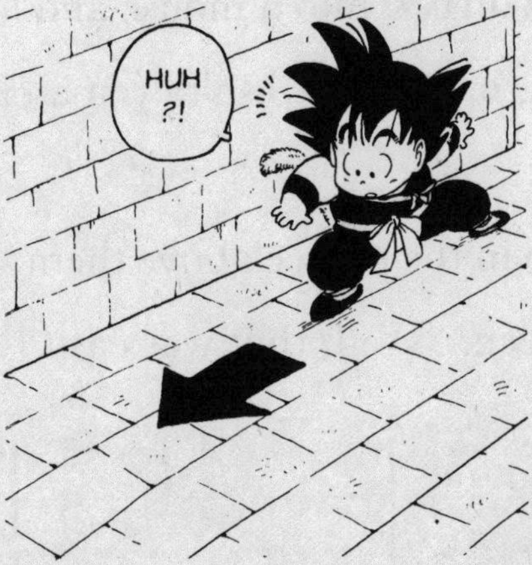
HUH ?!

"There must be something in that direction!" Bulma said.

"There's another one up ahead!" Goku said.

"And no one thinks *this* is suspicious?" Oolong asked.

"Follow them!" Bulma said.

"Huh, it's a dead end," said Goku, coming to the last arrow.

Suddenly, a stone wall slammed down behind them.

"We're trapped!" Bulma cried.

Goku pounded the walls, but they wouldn't budge. Pu'ar turned into a mouse and looked for any tiny way out, but there wasn't even a crack he could slip through.

High up in the palace above them, Mai watched on a TV screen. "Well, that was easy," she said.

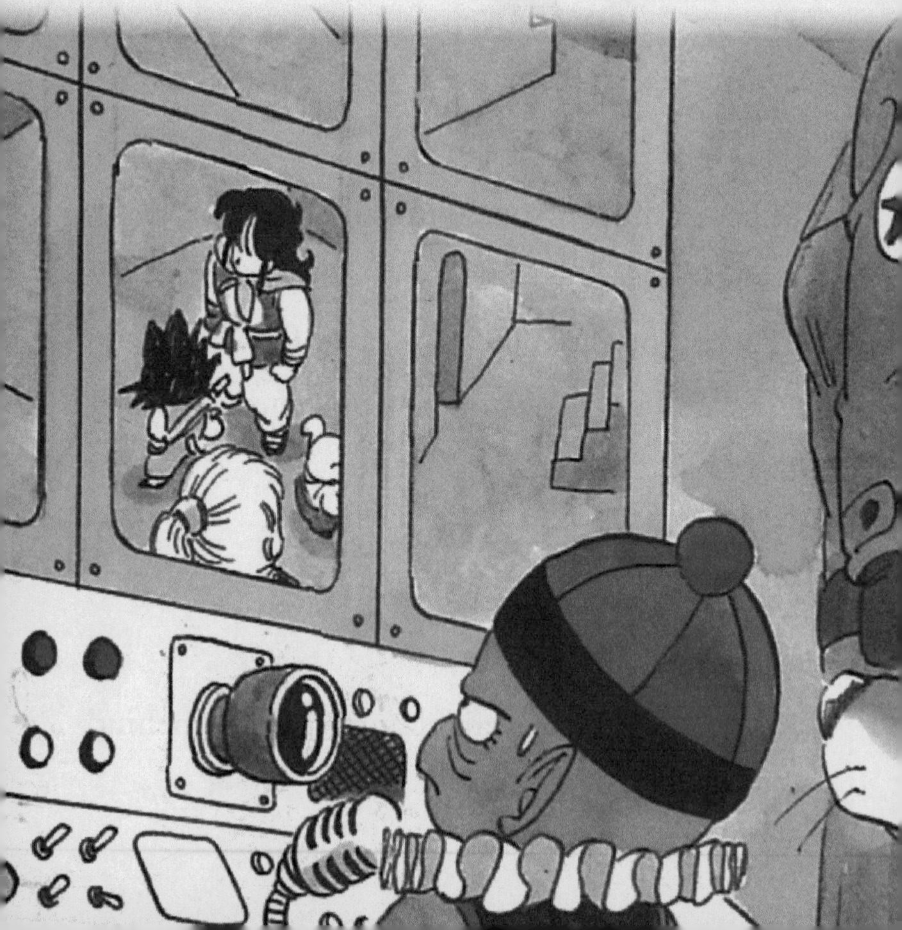

"I never thought anyone would be *that* stupid," Pilaf said, shaking his head.

Mai went to search Yamcha's car for the last Dragon Ball. She came back empty-handed.

"One of our captives must have it on him," she said.

"Or *her*," Emperor Pilaf said, watching Bulma on the TV screen. "That one appears to be the leader. Mai! I will speak with the prisoners!"

Goku and Yamcha were looking frantically for a way out of their dungeon when a wall panel slid back, revealing a glowing screen. The sour face of Emperor Pilaf glared at them.

"A window!" Goku yelled. "We can break through it!"

"Haven't you ever seen a TV before?" Yamcha snapped.

"Greetings, prisoners!" the emperor snarled. "I am Pilaf the Great...the next ruler of the world!"

"You're the one who stole my Dragon Balls!"

Bulma yelled.

"All but one," Pilaf said with a smirk. "And if you hope to escape alive, you will give it to me!"

"Oh, we'll give it to you, all right," Bulma yelled. "Come an' get it!"

A look of rage twisted Pilaf's face. "Fine. If that's how you want to play it, you leave me no choice. I will subject you to the most terrible torture I can imagine!"

Suddenly a panel slid open in the ceiling. Before anyone could react, a mechanical arm dropped down, caught Bulma, and dragged her back through the opening. The panel slid closed just as Goku threw himself against it.

"Let me go, you monster!" Bulma yelled as the mechanical arm delivered her to the emperor's chamber.

"I will let you go when you give me that Dragon Ball!" Pilaf said.

"It's mine and you can't have it!" Bulma said.

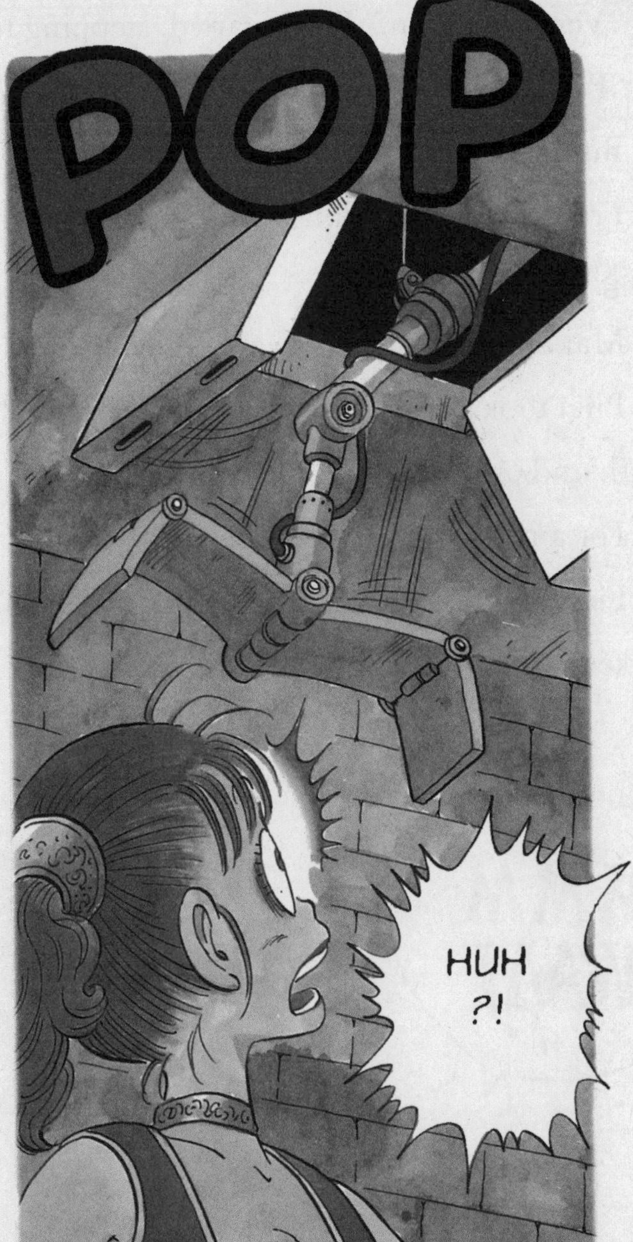
POP
HUH ?!

"Very well then," Pilaf snarled, stepping toward her. "Prepare to be tortured!"

Bulma braced herself.

From inside the dungeon Yamcha yelled, "Be strong! We're with you!"

Mai and Shu turned away in horror.

Pilaf took a deep breath, brought his hand to his mouth and–*MMMWAH!*

For a moment, no one spoke.

Finally Pilaf broke the silence. "Well?" he smirked. "Are you ready to talk now?"

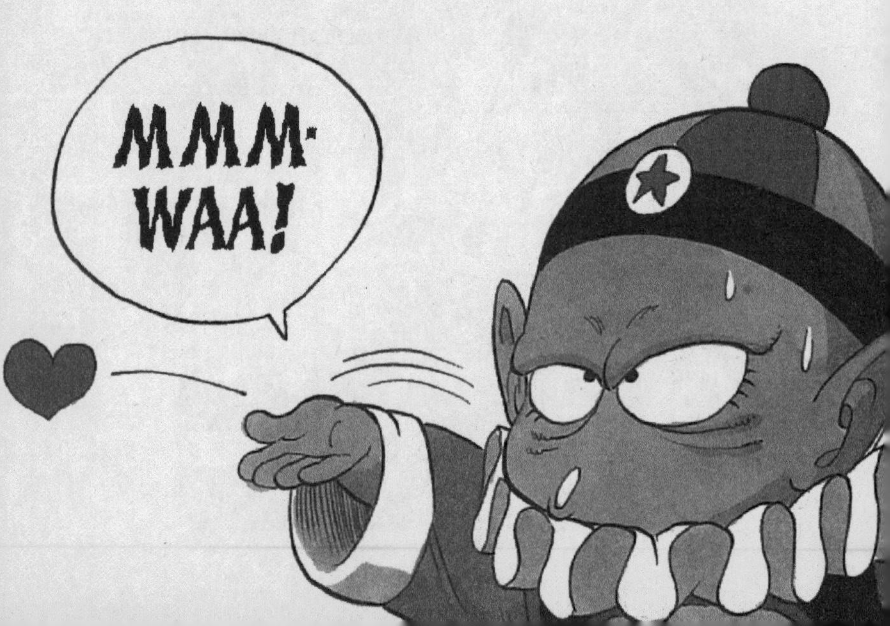
MMM-
WAA!

"That's it?" Bulma asked. "What *was* that?"

Pilaf was shocked. "I-I-I just blew you a k-k-*kiss!* What could be more terrifying than that?"

"True, you're not exactly my type," Bulma said, her eyes twinkling with mischief. "But believe me, there are far more terrifying things than a kiss from a pint-sized weirdo like you."

Then she listed the possibilities, including being licked by puppies, eating strawberry ice cream, lying in the sun on a perfect summer day, and having her ankles rubbed by purring kittens.

"Stop! Stop! STOP!" Pilaf cried.

"Mai! Shu! Send her away before she gives me nightmares!"

Mai pushed a button and the mechanical arm whipped Bulma back to the dungeon.

"Clearly we're up against something more terrible than I ever imagined," Pilaf sneered.

"How about knocking them out with sleeping gas and searching them?" Mai asked.

"Exactly what I was about to suggest!" snarled the emperor. "I'm glad that you've finally learned something from me!"

Back in the dungeon, small tubes pushed out of the wall and filled the chamber with clouds of gas.

"What's that?" Goku asked.

"Hold your breath!" Yamcha coughed.

But there was nothing they could do. Within minutes they were all sound asleep.

A short time later, a stone wall at one end of the dungeon rose. Shu stepped into the chamber wearing a gas mask. Mai followed, also wearing a gas mask. Then the emperor stepped inside.

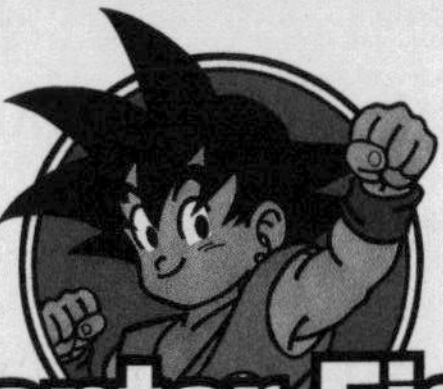

Chapter Eight

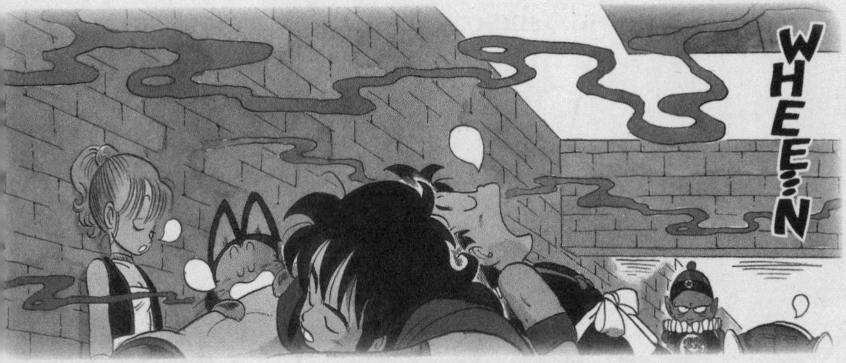
WHEE...N

"Mwa ha ha!" Pilaf laughed, as he stepped over the unconscious bodies of Goku and his friends. "Sleeping like babies! Now let's find that...that Drag...Dragon...Buhh...zzzzzzzzzz."

The emperor fell to the floor, fast asleep.

"Emperor Pilaf! What's wrong?" cried Shu.

"He forgot to put his gas mask on," Mai sighed. "Stay with him, Shu. I'll find that Dragon Ball."

As Shu dragged Pilaf outside, Mai looked through Bulma's clothes. No Dragon Ball. Then she turned to Oolong. No Dragon Ball. Next, she turned to Goku. She quickly found the pouch in which he carried the his grampa's four-star ball.

"I've got it!" she cried.

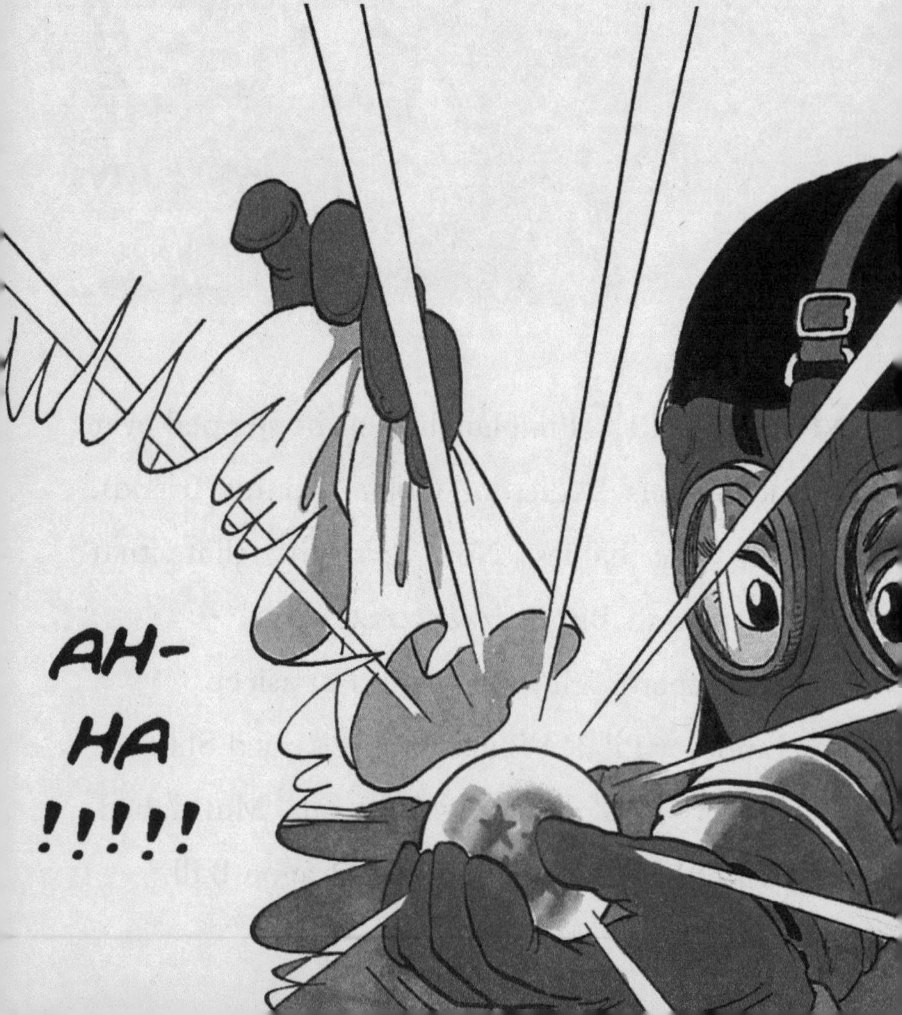
AH-
HA
!!!!!

Outside the chamber Pilaf was waking up. He heard Mai's cry and thought he was still dreaming.

"We've got it!" Mai shouted, rushing toward him, Goku's Dragon Ball in her hand. "We've got the last Dragon Ball!"

"So it wasn't a dream?" Pilaf yawned. Then he began to laugh. Not quite as evilly this time, but it was still pretty sinister. "Excellent work, Mai. Now the mighty Pilaf will be the most powerful being on earth!"

Back in the dungeon, the sleeping gas was beginning the wear off. Yamcha was the first to wake. The moment he realized what had happened, he shook Goku awake too.

"The Dragon Ball!" Yamcha cried. "Do you still have it?"

"N-no," Goku said, feeling the empty pouch. "They took it!"

"We've got to get out of here!" Yamcha roared, punching the wall with all his might. "We've got to stop them!"

"It's too late," wailed Bulma, who was awake now too. "That little creep's probably already had his wish granted! Our quest is over! We lost!"

"We can't just give up!" Yamcha said. "Goku! That blow Master Roshi taught you–the Kamehameha!"

"Oh yeah!" Goku said. "But how do *you* know about that?"

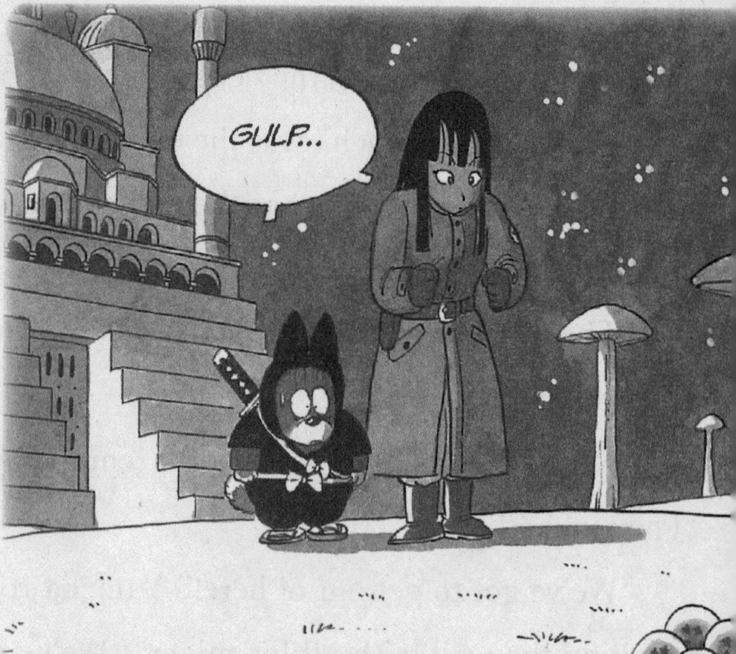
GULP...

"Is this any time to ask how I know what I know?" Yamcha yelled. "Use the Kamehame-ha to break down this wall!"

Goku nodded. "Okay. Stand back."

Outside, Emperor Pilaf had placed all seven Dragon Balls together on the ground. Now that the balls were all touching, energy crackled from one to another until a great glow filled the night.

"Get ready," Pilaf said. "I'm about to summon the Dragon God!"

Shu and Mai both gulped nervously.

In the dungeon, Goku brought his wrists together the way he had at Fry Pan Mountain. "Ka… Me…" he twisted his body and brought his arms back, preparing to unleash a burst of pure energy. "Ha…Me…HA!" he roared as he pushed his energy toward one of the dungeon's walls.

A flash of power shot from his hands and blew right through the wall!

Unfortunately, it only made a small hole.

"How are we supposed to get through that?" screamed Oolong.

"Oops," Goku said with a grin. "I guess I still need some practice."

"He's out there!" shouted Yamcha, looking through the hole. He could clearly see Pilaf standing over the glowing balls. "And it looks like the dragon hasn't appeared yet! Pu'ar! Turn into a bat! Fly out there and grab one of those balls before it's too late!"

"Will do!" Pu'ar said. He *POOF*ed into a bat and zipped through the hole.

"You're sooo brilliant!" Bulma said to Yamcha. She whipped around and faced Oolong. "What're you just standing there for? Get out there with Pu'ar!"

"What am *I* supposed to do?" Oolong groaned. But Bulma looked so angry that he said, "I'll do it! I'll do it!" Then he turned into a bat too and zipped out after Pu'ar.

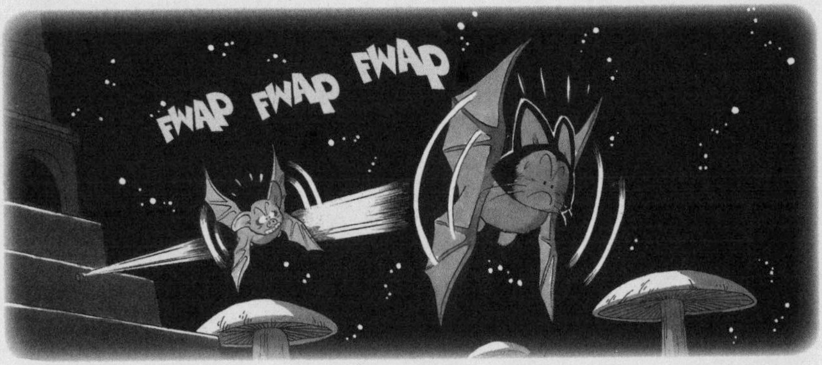
FWAP FWAP FWAP

Pu'ar flew as fast as any bat has ever flown. He saw the Dragon Balls just a few yards ahead of him.

He zeroed in on the closest one, knowing he only needed to pull one from the group to break the power of them all. He swooped down and stretched his bat feet out ahead of him to grab it...

...just as Emperor Pilaf finished the spell to summon the dragon: "Shen Long, come forth! Grant me my wish!"

Instantly the energy exploded from the Dragon Balls. Pu'ar was knocked back by the force. A great column of light rose into the air. It began to twist and dance as if it were a living thing. Then it took the *shape* of a living thing. Legs. Arms. Claws and scales. And finally, a great snarling head with glowing red eyes and a mouth full of terrifying teeth.

Shen Long had come!

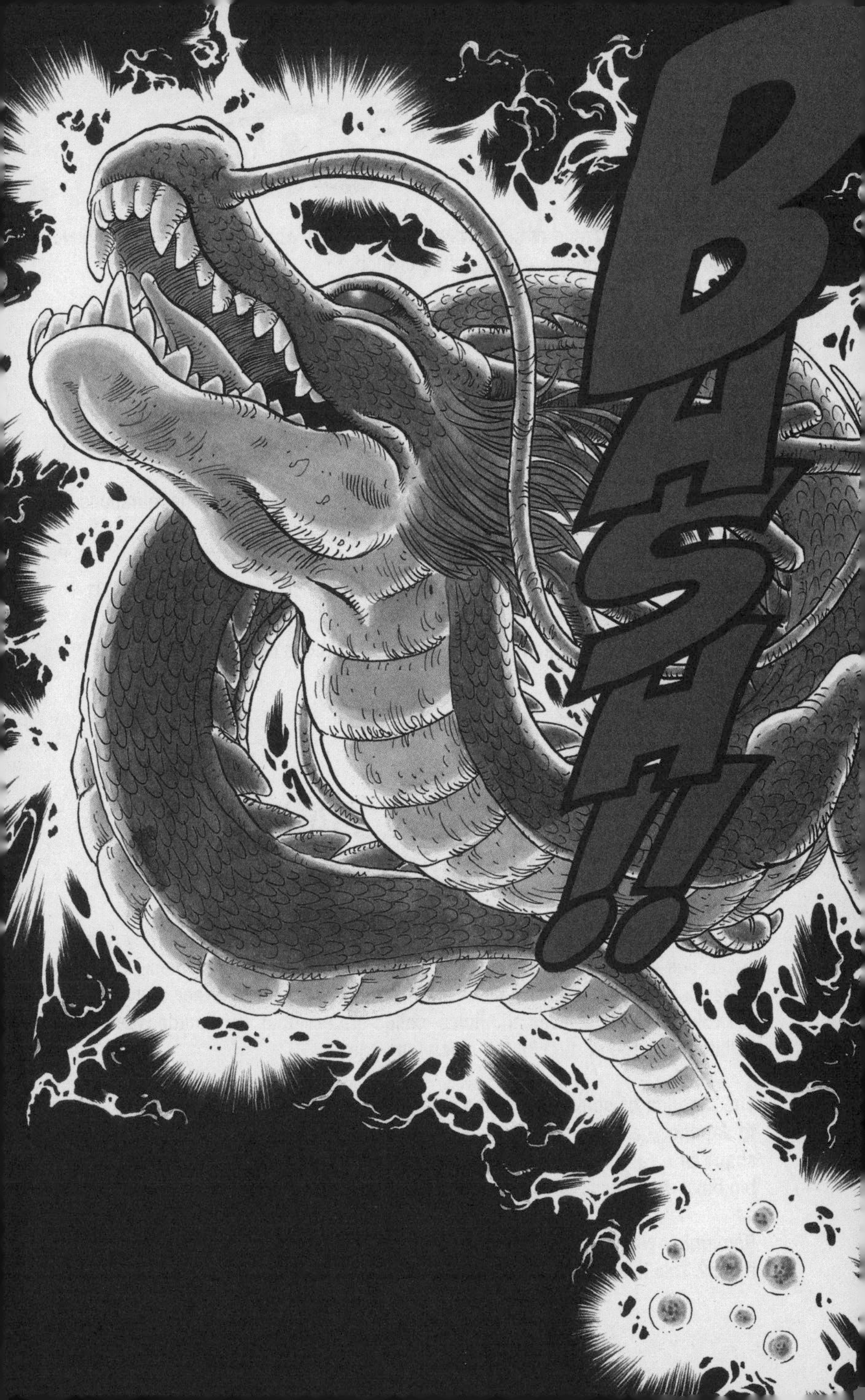
BASH!!

Glossary

Dragon Ball: one of seven mythical orbs that when brought together have the power to summon a wish-granting dragon

Dragon Radar: a machine invented by Bulma that picks up and tracks the energy of the Dragon Balls

Hoi-Poi Capsule: a tiny tube that holds any number of objects—including cars and houses—and releases these objects when thrown on the ground

Kamehameha: Master Roshi's signature move for which he summons all of his energy and focuses it into a single powerful blast

Kinto'un: a flying cloud that will only carry those who are pure of heart

Nyoibo: Goku's magic fighting staff that lengthens on command

A Note About the Myth of the Moon Rabbit

Have you ever noticed the markings on the surface of the moon? They're easiest to see when the moon is full. Scientists think that some of these markings were made from the lava flow of ancient moon volcanoes. Other markings are the volcanoes themselves and holes—called *craters*—that were made when rocks collided with the surface of the moon long ago.

The legends of some East Asian cultures offer another explanation. According to Japanese and Chinese mythology, for example, the moon markings form the shape of a rabbit. In just about every story the rabbit is making something in a big bowl, from a magic potion to food.

Remember when Goku defeats the Rabbit Mob and carries them all the way to the moon? This is a reference to the myth of the moon rabbit.

About the Authors

Akira Toriyama
Original Creator of the *Dragon Ball* Manga

Artist/writer Akira Toriyama burst onto the manga (Japanese comics) scene in 1980, with the wildly popular *Dr. Slump*, a science fiction comedy about the adventures of a mad scientist and his android daughter. In 1984 he created the beloved series *Dragon Ball,* which has been translated into many languages, and, as a series, has sold over 150 million copies in Japan. Toriyama-san lives with his family in Japan.

Gerard Jones
Dragon Ball Chapter Book Author

Gerard Jones has been adapting Japanese manga for English-speaking audiences since 1989, including the entire run of *Dragon Ball* comics for VIZ Media and the *Pokémon* comic strip for Creators Syndicate (reprinted by VIZ as *Pikachu Meets the Press*). He has also written hundreds of original comic books for Marvel, DC, and other publishers, and he is the author of several books on popular culture and children's media, including *Killing Monsters* and the Eisner Award-winning *Men of Tomorrow.* He lives in San Francisco with his wife and son, where he works and teaches at the San Francisco Writers Grotto.

Coming Soon...

Book Five
ONE ENEMY, ONE GOAL

Things are not looking good. Lord Pilaf has all seven Dragon Balls, our heroes are locked in a dungeon, and Goku is hungry again! Is this the end of life as we know it? Is Pilaf about to become king of the world? Find out in the next volume of *Dragon Ball*!

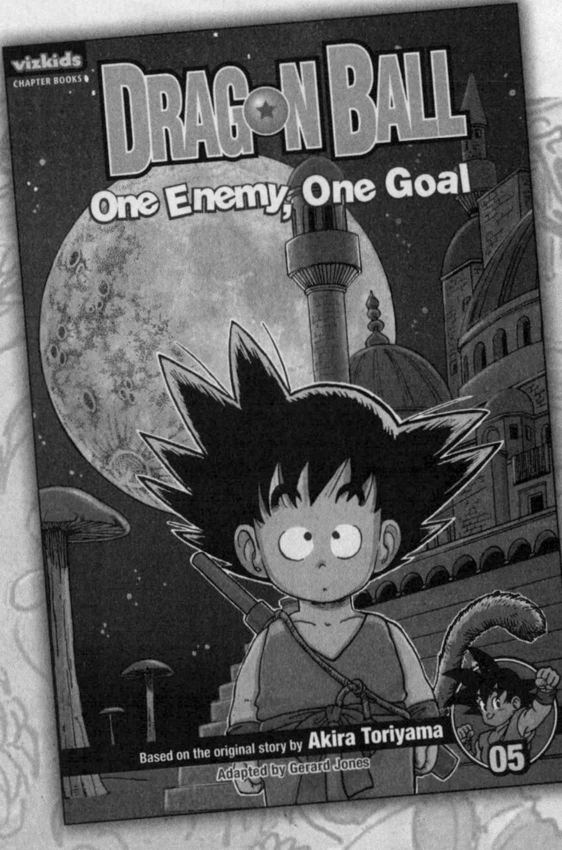

vizkids
CHAPTER BOOKS
DRAGON BALL
One Enemy, One Goal
Based on the original story by Akira Toriyama
Adapted by Gerard Jones
05